Ben paced, u...

She was leaving the ranch. He was soon to be rid of her. He should have been glad. And yet…

Looking at her, swollen with child, broke and alone, Ben caught himself thinking crazy thoughts. Thoughts he had no business thinking.

Dammit, he was a loner. It's what he wanted—*needed*—to be. So why in *hell* would he want to saddle himself with a wife and kid, even for a little while?

He didn't. But even so…

"Don't bother to argue, Marcie," he abruptly growled. "My mind is made up. If it's money and a name you need for this baby…then *I'll* be the one to provide it!"

Dear Reader,

This month we have a wonderful lineup of love stories for you, guaranteed to warm your heart on these chilly autumn nights.

Favorite author Terry Essig starts us off with love and laughter in this month's FABULOUS FATHERS title, *Daddy on Board*. Lenore Pettit knew her son, Tim, needed a father figure—but why did the boy choose her boss, Paul McDaniels? And how did Tim ever persuade her to let Paul take them all on a cross-country "family" vacation?

Those rugged men of the West always have a way of winning our hearts, as Lindsay Longford shows us in *The Cowboy and the Princess*. Yet, when devilishly handsome heartbreaker Hank Tyler meets Gillian Elliot, she seems to be the *only* woman alive immune to his charms! Or, is this clever "princess" just holding out to be Hank's bride?

Anne Peters winds up her FIRST COMES MARRIAGE trilogy with *Along Comes Baby*. When Ben Kertin finds Marcie Hillier, pregnant and penniless, he gallantly offers marriage. But Marcie longs for more than Ben's compassion—she wants to win his love.

Jayne Addison brings us a fun-filled Western romance in *Wild West Wife*. And don't miss Donna Clayton's *Fortune's Bride*—a surprise inheritance brings one woman unexpected love. And, in Laura Anthony's *Second Chance Family*, reunited lovers are given a new chance at happiness.

Happy Reading!

Anne Canadeo

Senior Editor

Please address questions and book requests to:
Silhouette Reader Service
U.S.: 3010 Walden Ave., P.O. Box 1325, Buffalo, NY 14269
Canadian: P.O. Box 609, Fort Erie, Ont. L2A 5X3

ALONG COMES BABY

Anne Peters

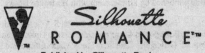

Silhouette
R O M A N C E™
Published by Silhouette Books
America's Publisher of Contemporary Romance

To Jan and Bob, Adeline and Alton, Darlene and Jerry,
Mickey and Ross. Without all of you, I never would have
come to know the generous spirit and rugged beauty of
Big Sky Country and its people.

 SILHOUETTE BOOKS

ISBN 0-373-19116-2

ALONG COMES BABY

Copyright © 1995 by Anne Hansen

Printed in U.S.A.

Books by Anne Peters

Silhouette Romance

Silhouette Desire

ANNE PETERS

makes her home in the Pacific Northwest with her husband and their dog, Adrienne. Family and friends, reading, writing and travel—those are the things she loves most. Not always in that order, not always with equal fervor, but always without exception.

MARRIAGE CONTRACT

I, ___Benedict Kertin___, being of relatively sound mind (though this deal does make me wonder), do hereby agree to marry _Marcie Jacobs Hillier_, my cousin's widow, in order to give her baby a name, insurance and a place to live.

I do not, however, agree to fall in love with baby or mother, agree to become a real father or husband, or to have anything to do with mother or child a year after the baby is born.

Bride's signature _Marcie Jacobo Hillier_

Groom's signature _Ben Kertin_

Baby's mark _____

Chapter One

Benedict Kertin knew the woman was trouble before he'd even clapped eyes on her.

It was late. He was dead tired. After a long flight from Jersey to Montana followed by the seventy-odd-mile drive from Missoula to his ranch, all he wanted was some much-needed solitude in which to rest. To heal. To start anew in the one place where he had always known what was what. Where life was still simple, where the course of the day was dictated by the rhythms of the earth instead of by the rise and fall of corporate stocks and the vagaries of international politics.

He was done with that. As he was done with women.

So what the hell was a strange woman doing in his bedroom, bellowing, "Hold it, buster. Right there!"

He would have asked, but a threatening "Don't move another muscle" froze him in the act of entering the room. A powerful beam of light hit his eyes, blinding him.

The woman said, "I've got a gun pointed right at your—"

And then she gasped, gave a disgusted "Oh, drat" and abruptly plunged the room into darkness.

Ben, bewildered, was still blinking against a kaleidoscope of glimmering dots behind his eyes when once again there was light. Blessedly *muted* light now, from a bedside lamp.

In the glow of it, a woman with a wild mane of flaming red hair stared at him as at a ghost and demanded, "What on earth are *you* doing here?"

"I might ask you the same thing." Dropping his bags, Ben dismissed the fleeting notion that maybe he had taken a wrong turn somewhere. Though it had been some years since he'd made the drive, and though he was tired, he was not *that* tired. "This *is* the Lazy H, is it not?"

"There's no need to be sarcastic." Visibly vexed, the woman tossed aside a large flashlight. There was no sign of a gun. Ben was pretty sure now that none had ever existed. "You know damned well it is."

"Well, that's a relief." He shrugged out of his bulky sheepskin jacket, which was stifling him in the heated house. Tossing it and his brand-new Stetson on top of his bags, he put his hands on his hips and regarded the woman with a dark scowl.

Dammit, he thought, she was not only in his bedroom, she was ensconced in his *bed* like a queen on her throne.

"Do I know you?"

"Well, of course you do." Eyes the color of rich chocolate snapped to his in startled surprise. "Are you saying you don't remember?"

"Would I be asking if I did?"

"I guess not."

"So?" Ben impatiently prompted when she simply sat there, suddenly looking troubled and clutching the quilt with both hands fisted beneath her chin. "Would you care to enlighten me?"

She eyed him and sighed. "I have a feeling you won't want to believe this."

"I have a feeling you're right." His head throbbed. His eyes were gritty. His temper these days was precarious at best. Crossing arms and ankles in a pseudo-relaxed stance, Ben leaned one shoulder against the doorjamb. "But why don't you give it a whirl?"

"I'm John's wife."

She was right, he didn't believe it. "John is dead."

"I know that." Sparks of a temper equal to his own kindled in her eyes. "We were married nine months ago. A month before John was killed."

"One month before. Hmm." Pushing away from the door, Ben sauntered into the room and planted himself at the foot of the bed. John Hillier, married? Not a chance.

"And was I there to kiss the bride?" he drawled sarcastically. "Or, wait . . ." He pressed two fingertips to his brow as if just recalling something. "I remember. I was the best man."

"Neither."

Ben thought cynically that a less disillusioned and more gullible man might be moved by the woman's sudden air of wounded innocence.

"A friend of mine acted as John's best man, and there was no one else at the wedding," she said, her voice husky and not quite steady. Her gaze, on the other hand, was. "We—that is, you and I—met two years ago. At John's father's sixtieth birthday party."

Chester Hillier's birthday bash. Ben frowned as, staring at her, some hazy recollections about that day separated themselves from the morass of wretchedness that constituted his memories of the past twentysome months following that party.

The woman had been his cousin John Hillier's date. Her unruly mop of curls had been shorter, and it hadn't been red. Instead, it had been a kind of purple, the color of ripe Italian plums.

He could remember Jane commenting somewhat snidely on John's penchant for exotic companions.

Exotic. Yes, that had been her. Flamboyant. An artist, he seemed to recall. He had thought her zany, but harmlessly so. The rest of the Hillier clan—usually at odds about everything—had been uncharacteristically united in their condemnation of her, however.

And of John, for bringing her to the party. Not that John had ever given a damn.

"Refresh my memory," Ben said. "You're . . ."

"Marcie."

"Marcie," Ben repeated, and rubbed at the pain building behind his brow. "Jacobs, was it?"

"It was, yes," she said, emphasizing the past tense. "It's Hillier now."

"So you say."

"It's the truth."

"Maybe." Ben gripped the bedpost. "Though you'll forgive me for saying I have my doubts. But leaving that aside for the moment . . ."

His tone remained pleasant, dangerously so, those who knew him would have said. But his gaze hardened and narrowed when he added, "What are you doing here?"

"Well, I..." None of the scenarios Marcie had envisioned with regard to the unlikely event of Ben Kertin coming to the ranch and finding her had been anything like this. He had seemed like a pleasant man that one time they had met. Imposing and—according to John—driven, yes, but he had in no way resembled the grim-faced interrogator that now stared her down.

Meeting his glare, she knew he would disbelieve whatever she told him, but offered him the truth nonetheless. "John told me about the ranch," she said.

Digging a hand into her tumble of hair and leaving it there, she glanced at the ceiling. "He said it was his."

"*Half* his, don't you mean?"

"Yes."

"And did he also happen to mention that the other half is mine?"

"Yes."

"And that this house is mine and always has been?"

"Yes."

Galled by the woman's monosyllabic replies and stubborn refusal to look at him, Ben's control snapped. His palm slapped the bedpost and made the bed shake. "Then why the *hell* are you in it!"

"Because," Marcie exploded, dropping her hand, sparks flying out of eyes that were hot and huge and angry, "*you* were supposed to be elsewhere, amassing your fortunes and doing your chief executive thing at that conglomerate of yours.

"And because, dammit, the blasted guesthouse—which *is* John's—is not fit to live in, that's why!"

"Not up to your expectations of...luxury?" Ben snarled, matching her glare for glare.

"Hardly." Her hands fisted and she smacked them down on the quilt. "The place is uninhabitable by anyone's standards. As you'd know if you had bothered to show up at this ranch on occasion."

"We'll see about that." Marcie couldn't know it, but she had just pushed a major button. Ben's feelings about the Lazy H ran deep. He loved every inch of the place. It had killed him to be away from it. But the sad fact was that his grandfather had run it into the ground and that John Hillier—long on charm and short on responsibility—had had other priorities.

And so, as always, it had been left to Ben to do what had to be done. Which, in this case, had been to single-mindedly amass a fortune and bail out the ranch.

And, in the process, lose every other thing he'd ever loved.

Ben turned away, unwilling to let the woman see she had touched a raw nerve, but more determined than ever to get her gone. He sucked in a harsh breath to get himself back in control.

"I'm tired, Ms. Jacobs." Which wasn't strictly true. Sure, physically, he was wiped, but for the first time in weeks his mind didn't feel as if it were mired in sludge.

It was the woman, of course. Buttoned up to neck and wrists in washed-out flannelette, her face flushed and freckled and her eyes spitting flame, she sat in *his* bed tossing accusations at *him* when he should be doing the tossing. Namely her. Out.

"This alleged marriage of yours..." he drawled, once more gripping the bedpost. "I take it you've got proof?"

"I certainly do."

"Could I see it, please?"

"*Now?*"

"If it isn't any trouble."

Marcie gritted her teeth at the man's sarcasm. "Well, of course it's trouble. It's way past midnight, for crying out loud!"

"Believe me," Ben wearily assured her, "I'm only too aware of the time."

"Well, then . . . ?"

"I can last a few more minutes."

Marcie stared at him in disbelief and finally admitted, "Well, it's not here. I keep it in a safe-deposit box at the bank in town."

"Along with the family jewels?"

"Lord, but you're aggravating!" Marcie erupted, tossing up her hands in frustration. Only to immediately hold them out to him, palms raised, in a placating gesture. "Look, I'm sorry. We're both tired. Couldn't we postpone this till morning?"

Still glaring at her, Ben had to concede that she did look beat. Dark circles ringed her eyes, making them seem unnaturally large. Which, he told himself, wouldn't necessarily have moved him, had he not been so damned bushed himself.

"Very well." He waved a hand. "If you'll just get yourself out of my bed—"

"What!"

Ben winced at her tone. "Do you have to speak in exclamation marks all the time?"

"Sorry." Marcie sighed, draping her arms across her well-rounded midsection. "It's just that stairs are difficult in my condition."

"Which is?" Ben prompted, when it seemed she thought she had made herself clear. "A fractured leg? What?"

She gaped at him in astonishment. "You're kidding, right?"

Instead of an answer, Ben gave her a hard-eyed stare.

Marcie met it for a moment, her expression nonplussed. And then, unable to help it, she began to laugh.

Which was when Ben, thoroughly fed up, capitulated. With a muttered oath he yanked his bags, coat and hat up off the floor and stalked from the room.

"Take the back bedroom," his alleged cousin-in-law felt compelled to call after him. As if she were the hostess and he an unexpected guest. "Top of the stairs, first door on the left."

All things considered, Ben slept pretty well. He awoke to the smell of coffee. His stomach growled. A glance at his watch on the bedside table shocked him. It was nearly nine. He couldn't remember the last time he had slept this late.

In a hurry to confront and get rid of the woman, Ben was showered, dressed and striding into the kitchen exactly sixteen minutes after first waking up, only to find the room immaculately tidy, but yawningly deserted. Aside from the coffee smells still lingering in the air, only the whirr, hum and swish of the dishwasher were any indication that someone had recently been there.

And now that someone was gone. *She* was gone.

For an instant, Ben felt let down, even curiously betrayed. So it *had* just been a cock-and-bull story the woman had handed him. So she *had* been nothing but

a fraud. A phony. An opportunist who had capital-
ized on the knowledge—gained from John in the
course of their romantic fling—that none of the family actually lived on the Lazy H anymore.

How shocked she must have been to see him. Yet
how calculatingly she had played her game, how cun-
ningly she had manipulated him into letting her stay till
daylight before beating a hasty retreat.

With his hands on his hips, Ben surveyed the room
and grimly thought, Well, good riddance.

Man, but it was galling though to find that the first
thing he encountered here at his supposed sanctuary
was the same damn phoniness and deceit he thought he
had left behind for good. Damn her for that.

Damn *all* women for the treacherous creatures they
were.

Angrily dismissing this latest example of feminine
treachery from his mind, Ben forced it, instead, toward practicalities. He was hungry. From the payroll
records that Roger Stevens, the ranch manager, sent
every month, he knew that old Cookie Nichols was still
on the job, feeding the hands. Though Cookie would
be surprised, even shocked, to see him—hell, they
would all be since he had sent them no notice of his arrival—Ben was sure the old bull cook would have some
flapjacks and eggs whipped up for the boss in no time.

About to return to the guest room to grab his jacket
and hat, the screech of the back door out on the porch
arrested Ben's step. As he turned expectantly, the
kitchen door flew wide.

Ben stifled an oath when the object of his ire, his
unwanted guest, bustled into the room, rump first. She
was bundled nose to knees into an oversize, shapeless
and disreputable version of his own sheepskin jacket.

She clutched a bowl full of eggs in both hands and her eyes, spotting him, widened to the size of saucers.

"Oh," Marcie said, taken aback by the sight of the man she privately dubbed her nemesis. She would have preferred to postpone this encounter until after her trip into town. "You're up, I see."

"You're still here, I see," Ben shot back, and adrenaline surged.

"Well, of course." Marcie set the eggs on the table and chafed her hands. "Where else would I be?"

"Oh, I don't know." Ben disdainfully raked her up and down. "I'd say on your way back to L.A. maybe, but you're not exactly dressed for travel, are you?"

"No. I'm dressed for warmth."

"Well, it sure as hell isn't for style." Ben banged some cupboard doors. "Where the hell is the coffee-pot?"

"The coffee*maker* is right there on the counter," Marcie pointed out mildly. "Would you like me to make you some?"

"There's only one thing I'd like you to *make*," Ben snarled. "And that's an exit, off this ranch."

"Gee, I'm sorry." Burying her chilled hands in the pockets of the too-large jacket, and not about to let him see that his deliberate rudeness hurt, Marcie forced a careless shrug.

"I'm afraid I can't do that." Her voice shook a little, and so she cleared her throat. "I've sublet the apartment, and anyway, with John dead, there's nothing there for me anymore."

Ben's gaze hardened. "There's nothing here for you, either, Ms. Jacobs."

"Mrs. Hillier," Marcie corrected.

Somehow, irrationally, it pleased Ben to see that challenging gleam rekindling in her eyes. Though he had taken care not to show it, he'd been disturbed by the slight tremor in her voice just before. It was one thing to fight with an equal, quite another to kick someone who was vulnerable.

"Prove it," he said.

"I already said I would."

"When?"

"This morning." Marcie hesitated, and then added, "If I do, will you let me stay?"

"Not a chance. I came here for solitude, lady. Not to play house."

He looked so implacable. Desperation clawed at Marcie and nearly made her beg. She hated him for doing this to her. "I won't get in your way."

"You already have."

For a seemingly endless moment, they regarded each other across a tense silence.

Ben watched Marcie bite down on her lower lip as if to still it. Once again discomfited by this unwelcome sign of vulnerability, he dropped his gaze to her bulky form. To break the uncomfortable silence, he said the first thing that popped into his head. "You used to be thinner, two years ago."

"And you used to be kinder," she countered quietly. Kinder and gentler, she thought, recalling the tenderness with which this man had treated his wife, the laughing repartee between him and John, and the playful way he had romped with his little boy on the Hilliers' lushly rolling lawns.

"Yeah, well..." Turning his back to her, Ben raked a hand through his hair. "Life has a way of changing people."

"And not always for the better, is that it?"

Turning, his eyes raked her from head to foot. "From where I'm standing, I'd say that's so, yes."

"You weren't always this cruel."

"What I've always been is honest."

"Well, so have I."

"I wouldn't know about that, would I?"

"No," Marcie said. "But you will."

Their gazes locked. For a moment it seemed to Marcie that there was a softening toward her in Ben.

But then she realized she must have been mistaken because he suddenly slapped the flat of his hand impatiently against his thigh and growled, "I'm famished. Can you cook?"

Marcie closed her eyes and took a deep breath. It was an effort to switch mental gears. She opened the refrigerator and used the act of carefully placing one egg at a time into the compartment in the door to hide her too-raw emotions.

"Yes, I can cook," she finally said. "In fact, since I've been here, I've been preparing most of the meals for the hands."

She closed the fridge door and took the empty bowl to the sink before turning to look at him. "I'm not a freeloader, Ben, whatever else you might think of me. I've been working for my keep."

Ben steeled himself against the fierce sense of pride that underscored her softly voiced statement. He didn't want this woman to resurrect in him all the gentler kinds of feelings that had once been part of his makeup. They had brought him too much pain; he had worked too long and too hard to kill them after Jane's betrayal to ever want them back.

And so he demanded, "On whose authority?"

"No one's." Marcie bit her lip, debating with herself the wisdom of confessing the truth. Her own innate honesty won, however, and she said, "Though I did sort of intimate to Roger Stevens that you were aware of my presence here and approved."

"I see." He had to hand it to her, Ben thought, feeling a grudging admiration for her spunk. She didn't back down.

"I needed a place to stay. And I needed to be useful," she went on, keeping her chin high in the face of Ben's uncompromising stare. "Cookie is getting on in years, as you'll soon see for yourself. He needs help and I give it."

"If Cookie's too old to do his job," Ben said, again with deliberate sharpness, "he'd better damned well retire."

"And do what?" Angry frustration brought Marcie's voice up a notch. The man was impossible to reach, it seemed, on any level. "The Lazy H has been his life. He has nowhere else to go."

Ben knew that only too well. And he had no intention of sending the old man away from the spread.

But neither did he have any intention of letting this woman know that a few chinks still remained in his armor.

Small children, helpless animals and the aged—to Ben they shared an integrity and innocence he would never be able to resist. Only a few people knew that, however, and this woman would not be one of them.

Coldly he said, "That's not my problem."

"But he was your grandfather's friend," Marcie persisted in an appalled whisper. "And he worships—"

"Look," Ben curtly interrupted, "is there some food to be had in this house or do I go to the cookhouse for my breakfast?"

For all I care, you can go straight to hell.

Marcie was completely out of patience. Finally warmed up enough to shed the bulky fleece jacket one of the men was letting her use, she worked at the buttons with hands that shook.

"As a matter of fact," she snapped, "Cookie's expecting you in the cookhouse. Fool that he is, he's actually looking forward to seeing you."

She struggled out of the coat and, her motions jerky, went to hang it up at the back of the door.

Turning back, she caught Ben gaping. "Now what?"

"You." Ben's eyes were riveted to Marcie's bulging midsection. "Why, you're...you're—"

"The word you're looking for is *pregnant,*" Marcie said coldly, thinking it sure had taken him long enough to catch on. "A condition of which, you might recall, I tried to apprise you last night. And now, if you'll excuse me."

Brushing past him with her head high and shoulders stiff, she hurried out of the kitchen as best as her swollen feet allowed.

Ben stared after her till the door fell shut. And then, with a groan, he dropped onto a chair. Elbows propped on his thighs, he dug both hands into his scalp and thought, *Good God.*

Once again, an event beyond his control had wrested the reins of his life from his hands. First Jane, and now this.

Feeling trapped, seething with bitter resentment, he muttered, "Dammit all to hell," and wiped a hand across his suddenly perspiration-drenched face.

Because the hell of it was that regardless of whether the child was John's or not, and no matter the truth or falsity of this Marcie person's claims of marriage, Ben knew with a sinking feeling in the pit of his gut that he'd never be able to bring himself to turn a homeless pregnant woman out into the street.

Feeling stifled, needing air, Ben surged up off the chair and strode out of the house.

Chapter Two

She should have listened to Cookie and stayed put instead of letting that insufferable Benedict Kertin irk her into driving into town on a day like this.

Marcie inched along the deserted highway at a creeping speed, her frozen nose all but glued to the windshield—or, at least, as far forward over the steering wheel as her ballooning eighth-month pregnancy allowed. Her fingers had long since grown numb from the death grip she had on the wheel, as well as thanks to the busted heater. She did not dare take her eyes off the road that was, by now, covered by at least two inches of snow.

On the other hand, her mind rambled on, Cookie had the tendency to worry too much, and it honestly hadn't looked like snow when she had left the ranch. The stuff had started to fall while she was in the bank. Her first reaction had been, Wow! It had been years since she had seen snow.

They had probably forecasted the white stuff on the radio or television news. But who had had time to watch and listen with Ben Kertin ranting and raving at her? What an aggravating man. Talk about distrustful!

Really, this was all his fault. But she wished she had listened to Cookie.

Breathing deeply, Marcie tried murmuring a soothing mantra. "Hummmmm...I'm very calm. Caaalm...caaalm..."

She knew from her extensive reading on the subject of preborn babies that a stable emotional equilibrium on the part of the mother was vital. Deep breath, slow exhale. Deep breath. Exhale. "Caaalm, I'm very calm...caa—"

Oh, hell, this wasn't working. She was as tense as ever, if not more so. Only a few more miles, she told herself, recognizing the bone-jarring pothole pattern of the road as the home stretch toward the Lazy H. Almost home.

Home. Ha! Not if Benedict Kertin had his way.

Couldn't you have made him wait till spring to relocate to the ranch? she demanded of God and all the forces of the universe she'd thought were on her side.

Though what was the point of her baying at the moon? It was already too late for wishful and positive thinking. Her fate was sealed. The man was here. And he wanted her gone. Period.

Maybe.

Marcie risked a glance at the envelope on the seat next to her. Her ace in the hole, the marriage certificate.

Surely once convinced she was on the level, Ben would—

The van fishtailed. Marcie gave an alarmed little yelp and, clutching the wheel, swung her petrified gaze front and center and kept it there.

"Pay attention," she chastised herself in a mutter. "You can do this. Almost there. I think..."

Squinting, because somehow it seemed she could see better then, she wiped the side of her hand across the fogged-up windshield for the hundredth time or more. Through the ever-thickening curtain of swirling snow, she thought she could make out the ranch's massive gate—two upright Douglas fir timbers supporting a third to form a portal.

Below it, she knew, though she couldn't make it out, hung a board on which was emblazoned a sideways *H*—the brand of the Lazy H ranch.

Oh, please, she thought, let this be it.

She had been driving almost blindly for the past half hour. Had she missed the fork in the road at the Cooper spread? Was that really a gate up ahead or just a mirage conjured up by wishful thinking?

A quick glance at her watch told her it was just going on two o'clock. Darn it all. She had meant to be home hours ago. Old Cookie was bound to be worrying. He was like the father she had barely gotten to know. And like every father—or grandfather—a girl dreamed of having. Concerned, indulgent, never too busy to give a kind word and a treat. Without him, these past four months on the Lazy H, these months without John, wouldn't have been bearable at all.

Not that anyone would ever know that. Marcie wasn't one to wear her heart on her sleeve. That was much too risky. Because people had a way of backing away, of taking off and disappearing when they knew you cared for them.

Her marriage to John being a prime example. It had taken him a long time to wear her down, to get her to admit that she cared. And what happened after she'd finally capitulated and married him? He had stopped caring and then—bang, bang, you're dead. No more John, but lots of pain. For Marcie. Always for gullible Marcie.

Who could hardly see now. Her breath inside the frigid van was steaming up the windshield faster than she could swipe at it with her sleeve and hand. Besides, every time she held the wheel in only one hand while she wiped, the van veered to the right.

Almost there, though. That was definitely the Lazy H gate up ahead. It looked very grand beneath its blanket of snow... "Yikes!"

Watch out!

Marcie wrenched at the wheel and slammed on the brake as a dark blur—a deer? a dog?—flashed across the road in front of the van. The van fishtailed crazily. Marcie struggled to keep some control. But it was no good. Slowly but inexorably, the VW slithered sideways into the shallow ditch at the side of the road.

It came to rest there at a drunken angle. Marcie, her hands still welded to the wheel, sat staring straight ahead in unblinking shock. Her heart beat so hard, her body shook with it. And then her hands and arms began to shake, too. The tremors loosened her grip on the steering wheel and, with a smothered sound of distress, she buried her face in her cold-stiffened hands.

Deep breaths. Deep breaths. You're fine....

It took a while, but at last she felt a bit calmer. She raised her head. The windshield was covered with snow, obscuring her vision. She became aware then of the cold, and as if to confirm it, her body responded with a violent shiver.

"All right, that does it," she mumbled. If she sat here much longer, she'd soon be an icicle. The gate was just up the road, the ranch not far behind. She could walk there, no sweat.

Getting out of the van was another matter, however, as she found out when she tried to open the driver side door. The way the van was angled, she had to push the door against gravity, a task that proved beyond her. She simply didn't have the strength.

Well, it would have to be the other door then, *if* it wasn't wedged into the dirt and snow. It was. When she shoved against it, it budged for only an inch or so. But Marcie, after some moments of contemplation, solved that problem by stretching out on the seat and pushing against the door with both feet. As she huffed and puffed and strained as hard as she could, the opening widened and gradually grew wider still.

The effort made sweat pop out all over her body, causing her to ruefully reflect that at least she wasn't cold anymore.

When she deemed the gap wide enough to allow her swollen body to exit, she grabbed up her shoulder bag and the manila envelope. It was too large to fit in the bag, and she didn't want to fold it and crease the marriage certificate. On her stomach this time, she awkwardly wriggled feet first out of the van.

She immediately sank into snow up to her shins. The tops of her boots only came to her ankles, but she had thick woollen socks on with the bottoms of her sweatpants tucked inside.

Using the side of the orange VW for support, Marcie made her laborious way out of the ditch that was, blessedly, either without water or frozen beneath its blanket of snow.

Yup, she thought, as she finally stood on the road, catching her breath, she was definitely no longer cold. She yanked the knitted wool cap farther down over her ears, tucked the envelope under one arm and both hands up into the sleeves of the sweater she wore beneath her serape, and forged ahead.

With her head down and eyes squinted against the wind-driven snow, Marcie withdrew into herself and shut out the world. It was an escape from the harsh realities, one that had helped her over many an awful moment. These days, though, she used the technique mainly to commune with the child in her womb.

How's it going, Widget? You awake?

As if in answer, the baby let loose with a drum roll of kicks.

Beneath her poncho, Marcie hugged her tummy, chuckling. *Okay, so maybe you won't grow up to be a rocket scientist. With footwork like that, flamenco dancing would be right up your alley.*

Trudging along, a soft smile played at her frozen lips. She patted her stomach. "I can't wait to hold you, Widget," she whispered. "We're going to be best friends, you and I."

So absorbed was she in visions of a happier future, that she didn't become aware that a vehicle had stopped abreast of her until a masculine voice roared next to her ear, "What are you, *crazy!*"

The sound had the effect of a cannon blast at close range. Marcie recoiled with a violent start. The envelope dropped, unnoticed, from beneath her arm. She blinked the snow out of her eyes and recognized Ben Kertin's forbidding face.

She barely had time to reflect that a good-looking man like Ben ought not to scowl so much, before his hand closed vicelike around her upper arm.

As soon as Cookie had told Ben that Marcie had driven to town, Ben had started to worry right along with the old man. Though for different reasons. It would be the last straw to have some fool pregnant woman do herself an injury on his account and on his land.

"Where the hell is your car?" he questioned, rage having replaced concern the minute he'd clapped eyes on her trudging along at the side of the road.

"It's a van," Marcie corrected. Attention to detail was the hallmark of the true artist, she had been taught. It was what separated the professional from the dabbler.

"What?" Bewilderment temporarily forced Ben into check. And then, with comprehension, he ground out, "What the hell difference does it make? Car, van or bus—what I want to know is, where *the hell* did you leave it?"

"Back there." Marcie gestured vaguely in the direction from which she had come. It was snowing so hard, her footsteps were already obliterated. "In the ditch. And there's no need to shout, you know."

"In the ditch." Ben stared at her as though she'd sprouted horns. Had the woman no sense of the peril in which she had placed herself? And the baby? "Why didn't you stay in town?"

"Stay in town?" Marcie was having trouble following this conversation. "Why would I want to stay in town?"

"Oh, I don't know," Ben drawled sarcastically. "See the sights, maybe take in a show."

Agitation made his voice grow loud again. "Or maybe because a sane person wouldn't be driving in a blizzard like this!"

"Well, there was no blizzard when I started out!" Marcie shouted back as her own temper reared its head.

"Oh, for crying out loud!" Aware—belatedly—that they were standing out in that selfsame blizzard, and that Marcie was quaking like an aspen leaf from the cold, Ben willy-nilly scooped her up in his arms.

"Hey!" she protested, once again startled. His snow-covered coat was unpleasantly cold and wet against her cheek, and she strained away from it. "Put me down! What're you doing?"

"What I should have done right away instead of standing here arguing with you."

He stalked around the hood of his four-wheel-drive vehicle to the passenger side. "Stop squirming," he ordered.

"Well, then, put me down."

"When I get you in the truck." He wrenched open the door and very gently—Marcie had expected to be dumped—deposited her on the seat.

The words of thanks and look of surprise she was poised to give him were forestalled, however, by the almost violent slam of the passenger door.

With a puzzled frown she watched him stride around the hood to the driver's side—a dark and angry man who scowled and growled.

But also a man who, for just an instant, had been capable of incredible gentleness. Maybe he hadn't turned into quite the ogre he pretended to be. Maybe there was still a way to reach him and enlist his support.

She returned the dark glance he sliced her as he settled in with as serene a smile as her cold-stiffened lips allowed.

His own lips thinned in response and he gave his attention to the heater, cranking it up to full blast.

"Are you warming up yet?" he demanded in a tone similar to that of a prosecuting attorney interrogating the accused.

"Melting rapidly," Marcie assured him solemnly. "And dripping all over your nice leather seats, I'm afraid."

"Damn the seats." Spots on the leather were the least of Ben's worries. Putting the Bronco in gear, he shot his passenger another glance, taking in the faded blanket thing that served as her outerwear, and the stocking hat that left only a small, freckled oval of her face exposed. "Don't you have a decent coat?"

"Nope," Marcie said cheerfully with a quick glance down at herself. "Never needed one before."

"Well, you need one here."

"This is wool. Wool is good."

Ben's lip curled. "What it is, is a joke, in this kind of weather."

"So I won't go out in this kind of weather from now on."

"Oh, so you'll stay inside all winter?" At that precise moment it didn't occur to him that he was still working on somehow getting her back to L.A.

Having finally reached a wide spot in the road, he concentrated on carefully guiding the truck through a hundred-and-eighty-degree turn that would head them back to the ranch. "This is just the beginning, you know. It gets worse."

"Does it." The prospect was daunting, Marcie had to admit, but returning to L.A. was out of the question, so she smiled. "Sounds kinda fun."

"It isn't," Ben said curtly. Lifting only his forefinger off the wheel, he pointed. "That your van?"

He didn't bother to keep the contempt out of his voice. The dilapidated vehicle, its exterior a mix of rust and orange, lacked only some Grateful Dead stickers to make it totally abhorrent to him. In his opinion, the kind of people who drove these vehicles were long on protest and short on ambition.

"Yup, that's it." Marcie started to chuckle. "I bought it cheap for the drive out here, but it does look pretty disreputable, doesn't it?"

Intercepting Ben's narrowed glance, she laughed harder. "Admit it. That's what you were thinking."

"I might have been, yes." Against his will, Ben felt a smile tug at the corners of his mouth.

Seeing it, Marcie said, "You should do that more often."

"What?"

"Smile."

His reply was a scowl and a flattening of the lips.

Marcie tut-tutted. "Wrong direction," she teased. "Up, not down with those corners."

That earned her another scowl, darker than the one before. They had passed through the Lazy H gate and were driving up the private road that led to the house. Ben handled the truck with ease, unfazed by the snow.

"You're feeling pretty frisky for someone who damn near froze to death," he growled.

"Yup." As much as the constraints of the seat belt allowed, Marcie angled her body so she faced his profile. She wondered just how much she dare tease this brooding man. He used to have a sense of humor.

She said, "Being rescued by mysterious Heathcliff types always does that to me."

"Really." The look that accompanied that single word could have flash-frozen hundred-proof rum. "I, on the other hand, have no use for people who needlessly endanger themselves. And others," he added, with a pointed glance at Marcie's stomach.

Her attempt at playfulness thus dashed, Marcie bristled. "I was less than a mile from the house. There was no danger."

Ben braked to a stop in back of the house and jammed the gear into Park before twisting around to face her. "You drove your jalopy into the ditch, lady. I'd say there's plenty of danger in that."

"But nothing happened."

"No thanks to your foresight. You had no business going into town."

"Well, you're the one who made me do it!" Marcie charged, incensed. "You're the one who just *had* to see my papers."

"Damn it, that was before I knew you were pregnant!"

"What's my pregnancy got to do with anything?"

"Everything!" Seething in the face of the woman's obstinate refusal to admit she'd done wrong, Ben abruptly killed the engine and slammed out of the truck. He was around it and opening her door before Marcie could even locate the handle.

His motions impatient, he pushed aside her hands which were fumbling with the snap of her seat belt. Briskly he unsnapped it for her. And then, as before, he scooped her up in his arms.

"Will you stop doing that!" Marcie pummeled his chest and tried to wriggle out of his arms, but she might as well have saved herself the effort. He was large, he was strong. He was determined to carry her.

And, truth to tell, for all her protest and struggle, a tiny part of her delighted at being in his arms.

No sooner did she realize this, she began to struggle anew.

Undaunted, Ben stomped into the house and didn't set her down until they had reached the kitchen.

Somehow, Cookie was right behind them, railing, "Dang it, Miz Marcie, didn't I tell ye not to go? Are ye all right?"

"Right as rain," Marcie assured him, adding a quiet, "now that I'm back on my feet," with a quick, dark glance at Ben.

"What took ye so long?" Cookie demanded. "It ain't but twenty miles t' Deer Falls."

"She put herself into a ditch and then walked," Ben growled, growing furious all over again at the danger to which she had exposed his cousin's unborn child.

It didn't occur to him to wonder why he suddenly had no trouble accepting the fact that the child was John's even though he still refused to believe that Marcie was John's wife.

"Walked?" Cookie smacked his toothless gums in agitation. He looked her up and down. "In *that?*"

"Yes, in that." Marcie yanked the hat off her head and, after tossing it aside, finger-combed her hair with angry gusto. Static electricity audibly crackled and made her riot of curls stand out in all directions.

She should have looked ridiculous but, watching her drag the serape off over her head and making an even

bigger mess of her hair in the process, Ben was struck
by the fact that Marcie Jacobs was quite lovely.

The realization had barely formed when he squashed
it with a glare at the clothes the Mexican blanket had
covered. A shapeless sweater hung to knees that were
swathed in ragged sweatpants. "You went to town
dressed like that?"

Marcie glanced down at herself. She was dressed for
warmth and comfort in one of John's multihued
sweaters and some sweats. "What's wrong with it?"

"Nothing, for a bag lady."

"A bag lady?" The words stung. She liked to look
attractive as much as any woman, but when you were
eight months pregnant and without money for a maternity wardrobe, it wasn't easy. Still, she thought she'd
been doing pretty well with John's things.

"These clothes are perfectly fine," she stated indig-
nantly. "And besides, they were John's!"

"And your bizarre idea of widow's weeds?"

Ben could have immediately kicked himself for that
crack when faced with Marcie's reaction. Instead of
railing at him, as he had expected her to, she paled.
Before she bit down on it, hard, her bottom lip had
begun to quiver. Her chocolate-brown eyes burned like
coals.

Ben felt singed by their blaze. But, much more
painfully, he felt something he hadn't felt since he was
a little boy—shame.

He felt shamed by the mixture of hurt and contempt
that vibrated in her voice when very softly, and with
careful enunciation, she said, "You, Benedict Kertin,
are a heartless and unfeeling . . . shell of a man."

In the silence that followed, their gazes stayed locked
for several, almost audible heartbeats, and then, her

motions jerky, Marcie turned. With her head high, she walked from the room.

Ben flinched as the door slammed behind her. Pensive, frowning, he pursed his lips and slowly swiveled his head to encounter Cookie's rheumy glare. The old man's eyes held an expression that echoed Marcie's vocal assessment. Without a word, he turned and shuffled out the back door.

Ben remained where he was, motionless in the middle of the kitchen, for a moment longer. His eyes lingered on the door that had banged shut behind the old cook. Feeling old and sluggish himself, suddenly, he shrugged out of his heavy coat and carelessly dropped it on the nearest chair.

He removed his hat, saw the discarded serape in a heap on the floor and bent to pick it up. He shook it out and studied its threadbare weave of gray-and-black stripes in disbelief. For a Montana winter, the thing was less than useless. It weighed next to nothing, and its scent...

Bringing it up to his nose, Ben deeply inhaled. His eyelids fluttered, his nostrils flared. Its scent was of damp wool but also, pleasantly, of... her.

With a vicious curse at his foolishness, he flung the garment aside.

On his way to the study, he passed a mirror. He slowed to eye his reflection with distaste. *You're a heartless, unfeeling shell of a man,* the woman had said. And Cookie's accusing glare had seconded that scathing indictment.

Confronted by his image in the mirror and despising himself, Ben thought, Well folks, I guess that makes it unanimous.

* * *

In the master bedroom, Marcie lay across the bed and stared with dry, burning eyes up at the ceiling. She wanted to cry, longed to be able to cry. Weren't pregnant women supposed to be weepy?

But she couldn't. Had not been able to since the day, some thirteen years ago, when a brief and very formal letter from a foreign government had informed her that her parents had been killed. Buried, not by their only child the way they should have been, but by an avalanche high in the Andes.

All alone in the world and without a dime—her parents had been long on love but perpetually short on cash—she had spent a couple of miserable years in a foster home.

Oh, the Millers had been kind enough, Marcie supposed, but at fifteen years of age, lonely and grieving, she had found anger and rebellion an effective palliative. The moment she had graduated high school, she had split.

Enter Roberto Vegada. Bobo, everyone called him.

A smile trembled at the corners of Marcie's lips as she thought of the man who had, literally, made a new person of her. She had come to Bobo with the help of her high school art teacher. He had seen promise in Marcie's work. And so, eventually and after a rigorous apprenticeship, had Bobo.

The burning in Marcie's eyes intensified, making her long once again for the release of tears. Not much taller than she but twice as wide and three times her age, Bobo Vegada had been splendid in his tirades whenever she had pulled one of her rebellious stunts. Which, at first, had been often.

"You wanna learn, stay," he used to tell her in that indefinable southern European accent of his. "You wanna be cute, vamoose. I got no time for cute."

Darling Bobo. If not for him, she would not be who and what she had become. A strong person—most of the time, Marcie amended with an ache in her heart—and a darned good sculptor. Not yet as good as her revered mentor, and certainly without Bobo's wealth and renown.

But still, thanks to him, thanks to the guidance he had provided and the schooling he had paid for, she was a well-trained talent who would one day come into her own.

One day.

With a groan, Marcie rolled onto her side. She hugged her pillow, thinking that "one day" wasn't soon enough anymore. She was broke, she was pregnant.

And she was at the mercy of a man who very probably had none.

A man who was distrustful and embittered. Who viewed her with suspicion. Who, without proof, refused to believe she was who she was, or that she had a right to be here.

Well, she *did* have proof, dammit. And she'd shove it under his nose right this minute and demand he treat her with respect!

Tossing the pillow aside, Marcie crabbed her way off the bed with a wistful thought for the days when she would have bounded and marched instead of creeping and waddling the way she was forced to do now. Not much longer though, she reminded herself. And the reward for her discomforts would be oh, so sweet.

She moved toward the dresser. Her shoulder bag and the envelope...?

Were in the kitchen, she realized after an instant of alarm. They were on the floor where she had dropped them to take off the serape.

She checked herself in the dresser mirror, smoothed down her hair, critically studied the sweater with its high turtleneck and the overlong sleeves. She tried to see herself through Ben's eyes, the eyes of a wealthy corporate executive who had daily been surrounded by well-groomed and immaculately attired women. And her heart sank.

He was right, she was forced to admit. Compared to them, she *did* look like a bag lady.

For just a second, Marcie wished she had a wardrobe of chic maternity wear, feet that didn't swell two whole sizes between morning and night, and hair that could be tamed to sleek perfection.

And then she laughed. Who was she trying to kid? Even before her pregnancy, when her size had been a perfect six and her feet still triple-A, her wardrobe of choice had been vintage and eclectic. And her hair...

Giving the tumble of curls a flick, Marcie wrinkled her nose. Well, her hair was a pain whether auburn, magenta or blue, to name but a few of the colors it had been. And long, short or a combination of both, no matter how it was cut, sprayed or gelled, sleek perfection was simply not in the cards.

The baby kicked, hard, and effectively snapped Marcie out of her uncharacteristic self-absorption. With a rueful chuckle, she turned away from the mirror, patting her stomach. "Thanks, Widget, Mommy needed that."

As expected, her serape and bag were on the kitchen floor. She bent to pick them up, mildly surprised by the fact that she seemed to have flung the serape clear across the room. And where was that manila envelope?

She shook out the Mexican poncho, upended her bag, though she clearly remembered *not* having put the envelope in it.

Nothing.

A growing dread accelerating her heartbeat, she took another long look around, even going so far as to lift up each chair cushion and the tablecloth.

Zip.

The truck! She hurried to the back door, remembered she was in stocking feet and rushed to her room to get her ankle boots. They were damp from before and her feet had swollen, but she struggled into them and hurried outside.

The blizzard that had only been fledgling earlier was now raging full force. The wind howled, driving both the fallen as well as the fall*ing* snow this way and that in dizzying eddies. Just past four o'clock, it was already full dark. The yard lights shone weakly and milkily through the heavy white curtain of snow.

The truck was parked close to the house. Marcie reached it in just a few steps. Yet she was chilled to the bone by the time she had made a thorough search of the cab.

Nada.

She trudged back into the house, shivering, slapping the snow off herself, and all the while thinking, wondering, fretting.

Inside the kitchen, she dropped onto a chair and, grunting, wrestled the boots off her feet with the help of her toes. Her gaze chanced upon Ben Kertin's felt Stetson, lying on top of the chair by the door.

And suddenly she knew where her envelope was.

Chapter Three

"**W**hat have you done with it, you low-down skunk?"

Drawn up to her full five-foot-two-inch height, Marcie came at Ben, seated behind his desk in his office, with both barrels blazing.

"I've heard of some of the sneaky, underhanded, deceitful and downright dirty tricks you business types use to get your own way, but I never would have believed the man I was told to turn to in times of need capable of pulling such a rotten, despicable—"

"That's enough!" Ben had listened to Marcie's harangue with growing consternation. After that tactless remark of his earlier in the day, and given their tenuous relationship, he was willing to meet her halfway, even try to arrive at an arrangement of sorts. But he was not willing to sit still for the kind of abuse she was heaping on his head right now. "Please get to the point."

"The point?" Marcie exclaimed. "The point!"

Quivering with rage, she leaned across the desk and stabbed at the air in front of his face with her finger. "The *point,* as if you didn't know, is that you stole my envelope, you rotten thief!"

"I don't know what you're talking about." Capturing her finger before it could poke him in the eye, Ben half rose out of his chair, bringing his face close to hers. "And I'm sick of being insulted."

Without releasing her, he straightened all the way, came out from behind his desk and, ignoring her struggles to be free, pulled her along to a cowhide sofa-and-chair arrangement.

There, he gently, but firmly, pushed her down into the nearest chair. "Now, suppose you take a long, calming breath and talk to me like a rational human being."

After a brief pause during which their gazes dueled and Marcie kept stubbornly silent, he let go of her finger and took a seat catercorner from hers.

"You mentioned an envelope," he prompted, to get her started.

"Darn right, I mentioned an envelope!"

Not at all inclined to be rational, Marcie would have popped up from the chair if her girth had permitted it. As it was, the chair was deep and roomy and she would probably need a hoist—or a hand from *him*—to get her back on her feet.

The knowledge only served to dump more fuel on her fire. "The envelope I went to town for," she spat. "As if you didn't know!"

"Ah..." Comprehension dawned. Ben relaxed in his seat, folding his hands across his lean middle and stretching his long legs out in front of him. "The envelope with the alleged proof."

"Alleged, nothing!" Again Marcie struggled to get up. She needed to pace, to gesture with her hands while venting her wrath and frustration. "Look," she said crossly. "Get me out of this thing, will you!"

"So you can grab the closest object and hurl it at my head?" Ben shook his head, his expression wry. "Not a chance. Not before we've had this out."

Glowering, Marcie subsided back into the chair. "If you'd stop playing games, we wouldn't need to 'have this out.'"

The baby kicked, a whole volley of fancy footwork. Marcie's hands flew to her stomach in an unconsciously protective gesture. "Now look what you've done."

Raising her eyes in accusation, she caught Ben staring. At her stomach. And he had the oddest expression on his face. Pain, wonder, fear and a whole range of emotions Marcie couldn't—was reluctant to—identify.

All she knew was that, suddenly, at the sight of it, her rage fizzled out like air from a leaky balloon, leaving her feeling deflated, confused and curiously sad. For Ben.

"I saw that," he whispered, his voice sounding rusty and not quite steady. "The baby..."

His spellbound expression reminded her, suddenly, that he was a father. That he had a young son. And a wife. It hadn't occurred to her until now to wonder where they were.

Oh, God. Marcie closed her eyes as she thought, Hadn't there been a rumor? Something about an accident...?

And then it came to her—Ben's son was dead.

Oh, dear God. Marcie's throat constricted and she pressed a hand to her lips. That sweet little boy. Poor Ben. She recalled how he had adored that child. No wonder he was so different, so hard. To lose a child— could there be anything more bitter to bear?

"How far along...are you?" Ben asked, raising his gaze at last, his expression once again carefully controlled.

"Eight months," Marcie said softly.

"You're almost due."

"A whole other month."

"You have to go. We'll find you a place."

"No, please..."

"You can't stay here." His voice still sounded strangled, and he noisily cleared his throat. Witnessing the baby's movements had brought Jane's pregnancy, their happiness and Kirby's subsequent birth, back to mind.

And with it the grief and pain that had followed and pursued him ever since, stealing the joy from his life and his work until, finally, he had come back to lick his wounds at the one place where times had always been good—the Lazy H.

Only to discover that there—here—too, turmoil and memories had found him in the form of this woman.

Was there to be no peace for him anywhere?

Ben took a deep breath, calling on anger to obliterate the pain, and then directing that anger toward the woman across from him. "Dammit, woman, we're miles from anywhere. There's no one here to care for you, to handle things if—"

"You're here," Marcie quietly put in. "Ben, I'm healthy as a horse."

"Dammit, that's not the point."

"Then what *is?*" Marcie exclaimed, her aggravation matching Ben's. "Now that you've satisfied yourself that I'm for real—"

"I've done nothing of the kind," Ben interrupted impatiently.

"You mean you haven't even opened it?"

"Opened what?"

"The envelope, damn you. The envelope with my marriage certificate."

"You're still maintaining that there is one, then?"

"You know damned well there is." Marcie clutched at her stomach, breathing hard. "So stop playing games."

"No games." Ben drew a deep breath. He wondered why the woman exasperated him so, and why he let her. He had worked hard to attain the facade of cold equanimity he presented to the world. Yet here *she* was, getting past it with no apparent effort at all.

"But understand me." In spite of himself, exasperation sharpened his tone. "I do not have your envelope, you got that? I haven't seen it, and frankly, I don't care if I ever do."

"Yeah, right." Though she scoffed, Marcie knew in her heart that he was being honest with her. It was there in his eyes. Darker even than her own and as compelling as everything else about this formidable man, they snapped with impatience, but never wavered as she took her time searching them for the truth. He truly didn't have the envelope.

"Well." As her eyes lingered on his in consternation and reluctant acceptance, Marcie grew aware of a strange mix of feelings. Feelings that didn't belong here. Neither in this discussion nor in her reaction to this man.

Thoroughly disconcerted, she quickly looked down at her hands. *Idiot,* she berated herself. *Get a grip. Leopards don't change their spots. This is Ben Kertin, dum-dum. The man who wants you out on the street.*

And who's probably waiting for an apology, to boot. Oh, boy.

Apologies didn't come easy to Marcie. She had never been able to make them with grace. And she particularly didn't relish apologizing to this man who already seemed to be of the opinion that there was no grace in anything she did.

But she *had* accused him of taking something that wasn't his. And he was trying to be decent about it.

"I, um—" She cleared her throat, staring hard at the fingers she was twisting into knots. "If you really don't have it, then I'm, uh, sorry. I guess I, um, must've dropped it while I was, you know, walking."

"I see," Ben said, feeling strangely indulgent in the face of her obvious chagrin and discomfiture. He was glad to be off the battleground with her, too. Whenever she got into a state, there was something about her that, for his peace of mind, was way too appealing on a man-woman level. Better to keep things polite and impersonal between them for the short time that remained in her stay at the ranch.

"Unfortunately," he told her, "if that's the case, you can probably forget about ever finding it again."

Marcie nodded without meeting his gaze. "Well, I guess I can send for another copy."

"Yeah, you could." His gaze, quite of its own accord, dropped to her stomach on the off chance that he would catch the baby doing another somersault.

But all was quiet and Ben allowed his gaze to roam over the rest of her.

It gave him quite a jolt to notice, *really* notice for the first time, how very small she was, how almost delicate. The chair in which she sat all but swallowed her up.

He decided that he must have been too vexed with her, with her presence and the havoc that presence was playing with his well-laid plans for peace and quiet, to consciously realize she had weighed next to nothing when he had carried her in his arms.

Too, she was such a firebrand and coming on so strong most of the time, it was easy to overlook the fact that she was just a frail female.

As Jane had seemed to be.

Damn. Damn Jane. He didn't want to think of her anymore. And especially not now.

Ben gave his head one quick shake as if that would help banish her from his thoughts. Dammit, he had buried her more than a year ago; he had torn her out of his heart. Did she have to haunt him still?

He had hoped to be free of her here at the ranch where there were no lingering traces of Jane because she had disdained ever setting foot on the place.

Too restless to sit any longer, Ben slapped both hands on his knees and abruptly stood up. "But like I told you," he said, deliberately curt once again, "your marital status doesn't matter anymore."

He stalked to the fireplace and poked at a log in the grate. "If you say you're John's wife, you're John's wife."

"Well." Totally mystified by now by the workings of Benedict Kertin's mind, Marcie stared at his back. She couldn't help but notice the solid breadth and tapering shape of it beneath the checked flannel shirt.

Or ignore the fact that he was an imposing man, darkly attractive, even, it seemed, to her who was as big as a house with child and thus supposedly beyond feeling desires of the flesh.

Ha. Marcie inwardly jeered. Whoever had started *that* rumor had obviously never met the likes of Ben Kertin.

A formidable opponent was he, among other things. Which was why Marcie could scarcely believe that after all the initial hullabaloo, victory would be this easy. In a way it was almost anticlimactic. Unless...

A frisson of alarm puckered her skin as she finished the thought. Unless she hadn't really scored a victory at all.

She took a quick breath to keep from hyperventilating. Lord, but she hated to feel like a supplicant. That thought, along with a renewed attack of anxiety, unpleasantly raised the pitch of her voice. "So, uh, does that mean you will let me stay?"

"No," Ben said flatly, but kept his back turned. He sensed that if he didn't, he would see things in Marcie's eyes that would make him feel guilty about his refusal.

Which, he reminded himself, was ridiculous since he didn't owe her anything.

Which didn't change the fact that the woman had a way of looking at him that invariably made him feel in the wrong.

"I see," she said.

And the very tonelessness of her rejoinder aggravated Ben more than a screeching tirade would have done.

"Dammit," he snapped, whirling. "You see nothing, do you hear me? When the point is you're not my problem. Yet here you are, in *my* home. *I* did not invite you. Nor was it me who made you pregnant. *I* didn't kill your husband. And I for damned sure didn't squander all the money John made.

"And I know he made plenty, playing foreign correspondent in all the world's hot spots."

He leveled a finger at her and demanded, "Are you hearing me, lady? Hell, do you get what I'm saying? It wasn't *me* who caused you to be at this pass. You did that. All by yourself."

"Not entirely," Marcie pointed out through clenched teeth.

"No," Ben angrily conceded. "Not entirely. John helped spend that money, of that I'm damned sure."

"You can be just as damned sure that he helped make this baby, too!"

Marcie was stung beyond bearing by what she took to be Ben's inference that her child was illegitimate. She pressed a fist to her stomach and matched him glare for glare. "That's a Hillier I'm carrying in here."

"Fine." Ben felt like a heel in the face of her distress. He hadn't meant to infer anything, had only meant to say that it wasn't him who had been irresponsible, so why should he have to deal with the consequences.

He ground out, "Convince the senior Hilliers of that and you'll have it made. They'd kill for a grandchild."

"Yeah." Cradling her chin in her hand, Marcie bit her lip. Tears threatened. After all the dry years, tears now! Angrily, she forced them back down her throat, but they stayed to thicken her voice.

"They'd kill for it, all right." She turned her eyes to the wall. "Me, that's who they'd kill."

"Oh, for Pete's sake." Ben moved his hand in an impatient slicing motion. "With an attitude like that..."

Marcie's head whipped around. Her eyes, raw with anguished resentment, burned into his. "They despise me, Ben Kertin. That's not an attitude. That's a fact. I'm not considered good enough for their hoity-toity family. Just ask them, why don't you?"

"Maybe I will." Ben steeled himself against the pain in her eyes, concentrating instead on the worry, which he interpreted to mean she had something to hide.

The notion didn't sit well, made him feel a vague disappointment in her. Which was ironic enough to almost make him laugh. For who should know better than he about the deceit and treachery of women?

Woman, singular, some remnant of objectivity inside him whispered. Only *one* woman's deceit and treachery was really responsible for his pain.

The woman in front of him kept her eyes locked on his. "You don't trust me at all, do you?" she asked with quiet bitterness. "As far as you're concerned, everything I've told you is just one big, fat lie, isn't it?"

Ben's silence and hooded stare were all the answer Marcie needed. Her lip curled. "One of my gender must really have done a number on you."

With a sense of triumph, she saw the blood drain from Ben's rugged cheeks. *Good,* she thought with weary satisfaction. *Now you know how it feels.* "Was it your wife, Benedict?"

Something flared in Ben's eyes. Something dangerous, cold. It made shivers run down Marcie's back. Wishing she had held her tongue, she balled her hands into fists, though in distress, not aggression.

Ben did, too. But to contain himself, and his rage. To keep from reaching out and shaking her for dragging Jane's presence into this.

It took several deliberate breaths to calm himself sufficiently to concede that Jane had been there all along. That everything he did, everything he was and had said for months and months now was courtesy of Jane. Jane and her betrayal.

And so he nodded, slowly, consideringly, and said, "Yes."

He managed a humorless smile. "As a matter of fact you're quite right. It was my wife. You see, she stole my son and ran off to be with her lover. And in the process, she got the boy and herself killed.

"So, yeah," he concluded, twisting his mouth between words in a way that likewise painfully twisted Marcie's tender heart. "You might say that my wife really did do a number on me."

"Ben." Marcie despised herself for what she had done. It wasn't like her to be meanspirited ordinarily, she didn't have it in her to cause pain. Even to those who were causing her plenty. "I really am sorry."

"Don't be." Ben didn't want her regrets, her understanding, her compassion. For the simple reason that he didn't want to be beholden, but also because he no longer felt able to reciprocate in kind.

"Just leave it alone," he said, turning his back both physically and figuratively. "Leave *me* alone. Better still, just please get off my ranch."

To Marcie, his words were like a slap in the face. Anger welled up to momentarily anesthetize the hurt his rebuff was causing her.

"Of course," she said. Her lips were so stiff from her effort to keep them from trembling, she could barely form the words. She hated it that her voice betrayed her feelings, but couldn't help it. "Should I pack my stuff yet tonight?"

"Don't be ridiculous."

Ben told himself he didn't care that he nearly made her cry. Honesty was seldom appreciated by the recipients of it. Yet, even at its harshest, it was the cleanest, and hence kindest, way to deal with most situations.

"There's a blizzard going on," he said. "By all means, stay till it blows over."

"You're too kind," Marcie said, wondering where she found the strength for sarcasm while also wondering where on earth she was going to go.

"Just so you know," Ben growled, as though he had read her thoughts. "If it turns out the Hilliers don't want you, I'm willing to rent you a house in town. We can talk about that later."

"Sure," Marcie said woodenly, though she was thinking she would have her baby on the street before she'd set foot in a house for which Benedict Kertin was paying the rent. "If you'd help me out of this chair now, please. I'm really very tired."

Wordlessly taking her hand and hauling her to her feet, Ben noted again how slight, how delicately female, she was in spite of her near-term pregnancy. He saw the grief on her face, the sheen of unshed tears in fatigue-shadowed eyes and he felt hulking and brutish.

Not to mention every bit like the heartless shell of a man she had so recently dubbed him.

It continued to snow all through the night. By morning, the ranch and all its buildings were all but buried. Though snow before Thanksgiving generally didn't stick around for long, for the time being no one was going anywhere.

Ben, up at six after a near-sleepless night, had made himself a pot of coffee and some toast and retreated to his office.

He had earlier telephoned Cookie at his quarters and told him to stay put. To not try to make his way even as far as the cookhouse until the snow had stopped falling and the hands had created some sort of paths between the buildings.

The retrieval of Marcie's van would have to wait for better weather, too. Which was just one of the reasons Ben's unwanted guest wouldn't be leaving for the next day or so at least.

The other reason was that he had spoken with the Hilliers. It had been a strained conversation in the course of which Ben had learned some interesting facts.

One, that Marcie had indeed told the truth. John *had* married "that wacky nobody," which was one of the kinder terms Jaqueline Hillier had used to describe her daughter-in-law.

Thanks to his phone call, Ben no longer doubted that Chester and Jaqueline Hillier had little or no use for their deceased son's "eminently unsuitable" wife. At one point they had apparently even considered a post-humous annulment of the marriage.

Ben had also learned that after John's death they had sent a letter in which they informed Marcie that they would take whatever steps necessary to gain custody of their son's child.

"What steps have you taken?" Ben, appalled by all this, had asked.

"Well..." Jaqueline had faltered. "I, uh, I suppose you'll find out," she then said, rallying, "if your intentions are to meddle in what is strictly a family affair.''

"But I *am* family, Aunt," Ben had pointed out. "And John was my friend as well as my cousin."

"All the more reason to give us your support. Benedict—" Jaqueline's voice had softened persuasively. "If you know something, anything, of her whereabouts, tell us. We mean her no harm. Quite the contrary, we only want what is best. For everyone. You do see that, surely?"

But all Ben had "seen," at that point, was uncertainty. Whom to believe, Marcie or the Hilliers? All he knew for sure was that Marcie was scared. Genuinely so. And that until she, or Jackie and Chester, or some other circumstance convinced him there was nothing to be scared *of,* he would stay as uninvolved and noncommittal as possible.

The phone rang, intruding into Ben's somber reverie. His clipped "Kertin" was responded to by an accented male voice.

"Yes. I would like Marcie Hillier, if you please."

The voice was a warm, mellow baritone. Pleasant on the ear. Yet Ben unconsciously bristled in response to it. "Who is this?" he asked almost rudely.

"Vegada," the man replied calmly. "And, I'm sorry, your name . . . ?"

"Kertin," Ben snapped. "Benedict Kertin. I'm the—"

"Ah," Vegada enthusiastically interrupted, "the generous cousin." He pronounced the word *coozene.* "I am Bobo. Perhaps Marcie has mentioned me?"

"No." Ben frowned. What was this "*generous* cousin" bit? Suspicions stirred. Could it be these two were pulling some sort of extortion stunt on him?

Could it be Marcie was at the ranch for reasons other than she needed a place to stay? Could it be she didn't like the terms of the will? The terms that stated that in the event of John's demise, his half of the ranch would go to Ben?

What if the real reason she was at the Lazy H was to stake a claim by giving birth to a Hillier on Hillier land? What if she was here to lay the groundwork toward contesting the will?

His mind racing with dark speculation, Ben clutched the phone as if to squeeze the life out of it. "And you are what to her," he growled, "if you don't mind my asking?"

"But of *course* I do not mind," the caller assured him heartily. "Is good to know my little girl resides in your good hands, yes?"

My little girl. Hearing Marcie described that way by this...oily voiced stranger, Ben experienced again that odd feeling of resentment. The other man's very cordiality grated and further aroused his suspicions.

"I, too, am concerned for her, you see," Vegada was saying. "I, too, am very *good* friend...."

To which Ben silently commented with a cynical, I'll just bet you are.

"Yes. Long time, you see. Is perhaps possible I could speak with her?"

"Hold on." Taking the cordless phone with him— and his resentments, too—Ben stalked down the hall to the master bedroom. Though it was almost noon, he had not heard Marcie leave the room.

Not that he'd been listening for her, he quickly assured himself while at the same time wondering just what this Vegada character was to her, anyway.

At the bedroom, his curt knock went unanswered. Hesitating only briefly, he opened the door a crack. "Er, Marcie...?"

Her name was not easy on his tongue. Using it, something he had avoided doing until now, seemed to subtly elevate their relationship to a more... intimate plane. An unsettling notion.

He rapped again, louder.

"What?" Her voice came from right behind him.

Turning sharply, Ben saw her standing in the bathroom door, and the sight of her made something move almost painfully in his chest. Wrapped in a thick toweling robe, she looked fresh scrubbed and wholesome. Her curls, still damp from the shower and gleaming like burnished copper, framed her heart-shaped face in enchanting disarray.

She looked, Ben thought with another painful twist in the vicinity of his heart, more like a Madonna than the Jezebel he would have preferred to dub her. But then, looks could be—and generally were—deceiving.

"Here," he said curtly, shoving the phone at her. "For you."

Marcie's eyes, wary and questioning, remained on his as she slowly brought the unit to her ear. "Hello?"

As Ben watched, scowling, a radiant smile fleetingly transformed her face in response to the caller's greeting. Ben's breath caught at the beauty of it—and the woman.

But as quickly as her smile had dawned, it was gone. Her face crumpled and she whispered a broken, "Oh, Bobo."

The hand she put over her eyes, shook. She turned her back on Ben lest he notice. When she spoke, her voice cracked in spite of her efforts to stay composed.

"Bobo, for heaven's sake, where have you been all these months? I really *needed* you. In fact I've been frantic."

Her voice broke. "I'm going to have a baby...!"

That was all Ben hung around to hear. It was enough. The situation was suddenly crystal clear. She was pregnant, but it wasn't John's child she was carrying. It was this Roberto Vegada's.

Nearly blinded with outrage and something deeper and more difficult to define, Ben stalked back to his office. Too riled up to sit at his desk, he paced back and forth, all the while damning himself for almost believing in her, and cursing the woman for being the predictably deceitful female she was.

But, hey, he finally reasoned. There was a bright side if only he'd care to look. After this, he no longer owed the woman any consideration. He could get rid of her, without a qualm.

He went to stare out the window. It had stopped snowing, temperatures were rising, but the day remained gloomy, thanks to the leaden skies that canopied the whiteness below. Melting snow dripped from the eaves. A tractor chugged toward the house, pushing a snowplow.

Good, Ben thought grimly. If this kept up, the roads would soon be open and he'd get the woman off his hands double quick.

Brooding, he didn't hear the quiet knock on the partially open door.

"Excuse me. Benedict?"

Turning, his dark scowl met Marcie's hesitant smile. It faded on seeing his expression. He noted that she had changed from her robe into another set of unflatteringly too-large sweats.

"Your phone," she said, extending the portable without coming any farther into the room.

"I also just wanted to tell you that I now have somewhere to go," she added as Ben took the instrument out of her hand. Their fingers grazed.

Marcie snatched back her hand and looked away. "Bobo has agreed to help me."

"Decent of him," Ben drawled sarcastically. So what did *that* do to his theories regarding Marcie and the will? It shot 'em to hell. Or so it would seem.

"Yes, it is," Marcie said. She didn't understand Ben's sarcasm, but then, she reminded herself, there really wasn't anything she understood about this scowling man.

"What took him so long?" Ben asked.

"He's been out of the country for nearly a year."

Ben folded his arms and said, "Ah."

Whatever that meant, Marcie thought, bristling beneath her cousin-in-law's prolonged stare. "Bobo is arranging to have an airline ticket to Los Angeles waiting for me at the airport in Missoula. I'll be leaving as soon as the roads are open."

"That *is* good news."

His continued sarcasm both hurt and infuriated Marcie. She swallowed a heated response with difficulty and instead said, "My van . . . ?"

"Will be hauled out and at your disposal, of course."

"Thank you." She turned to go. But then, thinking she owed him that much, she looked back. "Bobo and I are going to be married."

"Well, well, well." Ben felt as though he'd just been kicked in the gut when the rational thing would have been to feel relief. "So he *is* the baby's father."

"The baby's fa—" The idea was so incongruous, Marcie couldn't even choke out the word. She gaped at Ben in speechless astonishment for a moment, and then burst out, "Is that what you think?"

"And why wouldn't I?" Ben countered, thinking what an actress she was—all confusion and innocence hurt. "First the man brags about being your *very good* friend and now it's marriage."

"So?"

"So just how *good* is he, Mrs. Hillier?" Ben taunted, driven by an emotion he didn't dare to define and wasn't particularly proud of. "Better than John?"

"Oh!" Marcie's voice shook with a mixture of outrage and pain. What had she done, that he should think so badly of her? She had always known, of course, that the Hilliers considered her worthless trash, but she had thought that Ben...

Blood is thicker than water.

Angry with herself for even caring, she averted her face. Tears threatened—she never cried—and she bit her lip to make sure.

"John said you were his friend," she said quietly when she could trust herself to speak. "He said you were the man I should turn to in case of need."

"I doubt he intended that to include giving shelter to another man's baby."

"Roberto Vegada is sixty years old," Marcie said, and her voice shook with indignation. "He may be nobody to you, but he happens to be a world-renowned sculptor who has been my mentor since I was sixteen."

As she spoke, her voice had steadily risen. Now she whipped around. Angry sparks spewed from her eyes. "He was the best man at our wedding. Never has he been anything but an honorable friend. And you, Ben Kertin, disgust me for insinuating otherwise."

Hands fisted, she turned on her heel and walked away.

"Not so fast." Ben roughly caught her arm. "If I was out of line, I apologize. But explain this to me—if all you say is true, why would the man agree to marry you?"

In response, Marcie stared at Ben's fingers clutching her sleeve. "Take your hand off me."

She didn't raise her eyes until he had complied. And then she said coldly, "Unlike you, Benedict Kertin, Bobo Vegada is a true friend."

"That doesn't answer my question, though, does it?"

"Maybe not, but since I don't owe you any explanations and your math skills are obviously lacking, it's the only answer you're going to get."

They glared at each other, their gazes locked. Though the prolonged eye contact was unnerving on a maddening and inappropriate level, Marcie was determined not to be the first to look away.

They regarded each other across a long and tense silence. A battle raged inside Ben. A part of him wanted to believe her, while another part, the part that clung to the pain of his dead wife's deceit, urged him to let Marcie go, and good riddance.

"There is nothing wrong with my math skills," he said at length with a sigh. He brushed a hand across his eyes in a gesture of weariness, but continued to look at her. "If Vegada's been out of the country for a year and you're eight months pregnant . . ."

He let the sentence dangle to its obvious conclusion and, instead, admitted, "I don't know *why* I'm having such a hard time with all of this."

Marcie stood quietly, holding his gaze. He is hurting, she thought. And though he doesn't know it, he is lost. Every bit as lost as I am.

She knew an urge to reach out to him but suspected the gesture would be rebuffed.

Ben prowled the room. Stopped to poke at the fire. "I called the Hilliers, you know."

"Did you now." Marcie hugged herself against a sudden chill.

Tossing another log on the grate, Ben glanced at her. "They confirmed everything you said."

"Wow." Marcie was proud of her flip response. She thought it very convincingly disguised the fear that threatened to strangle her. She hugged herself harder, stiffening her spine, bracing for the worst.

"I didn't tell them you were here."

"Why not?" Relief was making her weak.

"I didn't feel it was my place." Ben straightened. "They want the baby."

"Tell me something I don't know." Shaken, Marcie put one hand against the wall for support and pressed the other to her stomach. "They said as much in the first of their letters. And then a private detective came snooping around. He talked to my landlady."

Why am I telling him this? Marcie thought, despairing. *He doesn't care. Look at him and what do you see? A man, chiseled from stone.*

She glanced away, but kept on talking. "That's why I ran. And came here. And it's one of the reasons I'm marrying Bobo. He is willing to give the baby his name, to claim it as his. Later on, when the dust has settled, we'll get a quiet divorce. Ben..."

At the sound of his name, Ben looked at her. Her face was haggard and pale, but set in lines of harsh determination as she said, "The Hilliers will *not* get my baby. You know the kind of childhood John had."

Ben did know. There had been no warmth in the Hillier household. He paced, restless, unsettled, upset. Instead of being glad that he was soon to be rid of her, he worried some niggling sense of guilt like a dog worrying a bone.

She was leaving, she was no longer even remotely his concern. And yet...

"You said that anonymity for the baby was one of the reasons you'll marry Vegada," he said and had to force himself to sound offhand. "Care to tell me what the other one is?"

"Simple. I'm broke." Marcie's mouth twisted in a self-deprecating parody of a smile. She wasn't proud of the careless way she and John had lived, but at this point she couldn't afford to be coy.

"As you so eloquently pointed out during one of our earlier discussions, neither John nor I were any good with money. Still, I did think that Bobo, as my employer, had taken out medical insurance for me. Which was why I've been so frantic to reach him. I had to find out."

"And?" Ben prompted.

She shrugged. "I found out."

"No insurance," Ben said.

"You got it."

A strained sort of silence fell between them after that. Looking at her, swollen with child, broke and alone and about to marry a stranger, Ben caught himself thinking all sorts of crazy thoughts. Thoughts that didn't make sense and that he had no business thinking. But which refused to go away.

"Helluva reason to marry," he said, grimly kicking at a fold in the rug by the hearth. "Insurance."

Marcie said nothing. What was there to say?

"What does a sixty-year-old bachelor know about babies?" Ben asked.

"About as much as I do," Marcie replied with a choked little laugh. Much as she revered Bobo, marrying him held no great appeal. He would give her his name and his money, but he would not stick around for a minute to play proud papa.

Ben scowled out the window. It was raining hard out there. All the wetness was turning the snow into slush.

Which must be what his brain had turned into, too, he thought grimly, to judge by the stuff he was thinking. Dammit, he was a loner. It's what he wanted to be. *Needed* to be.

So why in the *hell* would he want to saddle himself with a wife and kid, even for just a little while? He didn't, but even so...

"Marcie." He spun to glower at her and she stared back in confusion.

"Don't bother to argue with me," he warned, "because my mind is made up. If it's insurance and a name you need for this baby, then *I* will be the one to provide it."

Chapter Four

After that heart-stopping pronouncement, delivered though it was in a less-than-heart-stopping tone and manner, everything had happened with lightning speed.

A week later, and married now for two hours, Marcie's head still reeled. How had it happened? Had she really said yes? Had Ben really even asked?

In retrospect, it was all one gigantic blur.

Despite Ben's warning, Marcie remembered protesting. "No way, Ben Kertin! You don't want to marry *me!*"

To which Ben had replied with a grim "Damn straight I don't."

But he had immediately followed that up with an equally grim "But neither will I allow some stranger to take care of family business. And it's not like it'll be forever, now is it?"

Heaven forbid, Marcie thought. They had agreed that one year ought to do it.

Documents to that effect had been drawn up and signed, along with a prenuptial agreement and a statement from Marcie relinquishing any and all present or future claims on the Lazy H ranch, with the exception of the guesthouse.

Since she had never had designs on any part of the ranch, and certainly didn't want Benedict Kertin's money except as it pertained to her immediate needs with regard to the baby, Marcie had no qualms about complying with all of Ben's demands.

Nor was she bothered by Ben's rather cold-blooded reason for marrying her—filial duty. After all, she had only chosen Ben over Bobo because she had a feeling that, given a choice, John would have preferred it that way.

What had bothered her was the way Ben treated her during the period between "proposal" and wedding. Or, more correctly, *didn't* treat her. For the fact was he had barely even acknowledged her presence. It was as if once he had done what he thought needed to be done, he had washed his hands of her and withdrawn into his shell.

Though she still did the cooking most of the time, he ate all of his meals either in his study on a tray, or in the cookhouse with Roger Stevens and the men.

He spent his days refamiliarizing himself with every aspect of Montana cattle ranching and his evenings in the study, either poring over books or glued to the computer.

Marcie was left to her own devices and spent her days pretty much the same way she had before Benedict Kertin had arrived on the scene.

And now she was his wife, a fact that delighted Cookie Nichols. He, along with ranch manager Roger

Stevens, had stood up with them at the strictly no-frills ceremony a surprisingly young and nervous local justice by the name of Claymore had performed.

Everything had gone off without a hitch. Everything but the kiss at the end.

Somehow, as they turned to each other in response to the justice's solemn "You may kiss the bride," their gazes had gotten tangled up.

They had gazed at each other for what had seemed like an eternity and the silence between and all around them had become so charged, it fairly crackled.

Something alive and painful in Ben's night-black eyes had touched Marcie's tender heart. As was her way, she gave in to the impulse to touch without thought of consequences and gently laid her hand along the curve of his jaw.

Ben had flinched, but not recoiled, and as he stared at her, some powerful emotion had briefly contorted his somber expression. And then, with a groan, he had pulled her into his arms and given her his kiss.

Not the chaste, perfunctory bridegroom's kiss the occasion and the nature of their relationship called for, however. On the contrary.

To the delight of those assembled, and the breathless surprise of his bride, he had kissed Marcie like a starving man. Like a man too long alone, like a man who had seen the depths of hell and now sought just a glimpse of heaven, he claimed her lips and feasted.

Not sweetly, but ferociously, greedily. And then tenderly. It was the tenderness that had made Marcie weak. That made her open to him. And offer to him, for just that moment, all the wealth of compassion and caring she had it in her to give.

For just an instant it was magic. For just a heart-beat they were one. And then it was over.

Ben almost roughly set her away from him and, his expression as bleak as the winter prairie, muttered something that might have been an apology or a curse.

And then he strode from the room, leaving Marcie and the rest of the "wedding party" to gaze at each other in uneasy silence.

Remembering, reliving again those brief, magical moments, Marcie touched her stomach and sighed. "He's a troubled man, Widget," she whispered. "I wish there was a way we could reach him, you and I."

They had been married three days. Thanksgiving was only a week away. Marcie had learned through consultations with Cookie that most of the hands had no families nearby and that it was customary to serve them up a Thanksgiving feast.

With her due date only two weeks away, it had taken considerable stubbornness on her part to get Cookie to agree to let her help with the making of pies and sweet potato casseroles.

She felt fine, more energetic than ever. She had even begun work on the guesthouse, which she hoped to transform into a dream cottage where she and her child could come and find refuge from wherever and what-ever in the years ahead.

Every day, book in hand, she did her prenatal exercises in the living room. Today was no exception.

She had finished her warm-up and was well launched into her routine, counting, "... twenty-eight, twenty-nine, thirty," before collapsing with a heartfelt "Phew," to catch her breath.

Which was when Ben walked into the room to find Marcie, panting, flat on her back on the floor.

"What the hell?"

Gripped by panic, he rushed over to her. Dropping to his knees beside her, he worriedly scanned her perspiring face, noting her heightened color and shortness of breath. He took her hand in both of his. A man of action, his only question was "What can I do?"

"Uh...nothing." Marcie stared up at Ben, both bewildered and embarrassed by his concern. "I'm just doing my exercises."

With her free hand she groped for the book that was her guide to preparing for an easier delivery through exercises and relaxation, regulated breathing and the strengthening of abdominal muscles. She held it out to him. "Here."

Weak with relief and feeling foolish, Ben immediately released her hand. He sat back on his heels and scanned the book while struggling to regain his emotional equilibrium. As was his way, he disguised the concern he had felt with gruffness.

"This says you're supposed to be working with a partner," he charged with a dark frown.

"No kidding." As she struggled to sit up, Marcie felt as awkward as a beetle trapped on its back with arms and legs flailing ineffectually.

Noting her predicament, Ben took her by the arm and, now that he knew there was no crisis, matter-of-factly hauled her into an upright position.

"Thanks," Marcie muttered before getting back to Ben's question. "And in case it escaped your notice, I have no partner."

"Had." Ben had a feeling he was going to kick himself for making even more of a commitment than he had already allowed himself to make by marrying her. But he went on anyway, saying, "You *had* no partner. You do now."

"I do?" Her eyes linked to his, Marcie swallowed uneasily. Did he mean what she thought he meant? And if so, did she want him to do what she thought he meant to? Namely act as her coach with these exercises?

Did she want him to see her, ungainly and awkward, while she struggled through the required routines with all the grace of an asthmatic beached whale? Did she really want him to touch her and...? Nuh-uh.

"Um." She gulped. "You're very kind, but—"

"Save it," he interrupted curtly. It seemed he would have to make his motives clear to her, he thought, since she seemed to think he was trying to be *kind*. Even in his mind he spat the word. "This is strictly about practicality and self-preservation. You're bound to injure yourself, flailing around on the floor without supervision. I don't have time for that."

"You don't have time for this, either." By now, Marcie was used to Ben's often brusque and insensitive manner, which she suspected he used to keep people at arm's length. But she chose to take offense to it just the same, snapping, "So don't do me any favors, all right?"

As if he would. Ben glowered at her. "I will make time."

"Not on my account," Marcie sniffed.

He ignored that as, book in hand, he got to his feet and then reached to help Marcie up, as well. "Give me a chance to familiarize myself with this text and we'll begin our sessions tomorrow. When is the baby due now, by the way?"

"December fifth."

"The fifth?" Ben paled. "Why, that's only...!"

"Two weeks away."

"Two weeks." Ben looked sick, something Marcie found vastly amusing. Men, she inwardly scoffed, always acted so tough until real life got into the picture.

"Should you be doing these...?" Ben gestured with the book.

"Oh, sure." Biting her cheeks to keep from grinning—it did her heart good to see *him* quake for a change—Marcie nodded. "No problem."

"No problem." Ben repeated the words in a doubtful tone. He decided to check on that himself. "The name of your doctor is?"

"Miller. Why?"

"Don't you think I should know how and where to reach him?" Ben considered that a reasonable question.

Marcie did, too, surprising him. He had half expected an argument, had maybe even looked forward to one. Always aware of her presence, regardless of where in the house he happened to be, he was wound tight as a spring and ready to snap.

But Marcie only said, "I'll get his number to you first thing."

"Good..." His brooding gaze went to hers and lingered there. Then it dropped to her lips and lingered there, too.

Beneath his scrutiny, Marcie's mouth went desert dry. She needed badly to moisten her lips.

Or else lean forward and press them to his.

Shocked by the errant thought as much as by the inappropriate longing that accompanied it, Marcie jerked her face aside.

She heard Ben clear his throat before, with a terse "Tomorrow at three" he slammed out of the room.

Only then did she release the breath she'd been holding as she buried her burning face in hands that shook.

They were in the middle of their first joint exercise session when the phone rang. Ben had been cueing Marcie's panting and blowing.

He told her, "Take five," and picked up the cordless phone he still hadn't gotten out of the habit of carrying everywhere. "Kertin."

Marcie lay on her back and caught her breath. She was feeling surprisingly at ease with Ben and his coaching; his impersonal attitude and handling of her had made embarrassment impossible.

Now, watching and listening while trying not to be blatant about it, she saw his brows crease. She caught the quick, troubled glance he tossed her as he drawled a lazy "Well, hello there."

A woman.

Inexplicably, the certainty of this hit Marcie like a punch in the stomach. She scrambled to sit up, angrily eschewing the helping hand Ben absently extended.

He was saying, "Nothing important. How about you?"

To which Marcie added a snort as she awkwardly regained her feet, knocking aside his extended hand and muttering that it sure was nice to know he considered her exercises "nothing important."

Thoroughly miffed, she waddled off in the direction of the bathroom. Again. Widget seemed to take delight these days in using her mother's bladder as her personal trampoline.

Ben's shocked "You're *what?*" stopped her at the door. Turning to questioningly look back, she was surprised to see Ben making urgent hand motions that indicated he wanted her to stay.

"Tomorrow?" he said into the phone while his eyes clung to Marcie's with something she could have sworn was desperation. "You are? In Missoula?"

Ben closed his eyes, massaging his forehead. "Yes, Rosalie." His chuckle had a hollow ring to it. "You certainly *have* managed to surprise me. Ha-ha-ha . . ."

Marcie rolled her eyes at his phony chuckle while at the same time trying to imagine what the genuine article would do for his face when even this counterfeit made it so startlingly handsome.

She had never seen him laugh, she mused, saddened. Nor even wholeheartedly smile. But then, his heart wasn't whole, was it?

And wasn't she the foolish one for wishing she could make it so.

". . . my wife and I will be glad to have you," he was saying, startling Marcie out of her momentary lapse. *My wife and I.*

It occurred to her that John had never referred to them in that way.

It sounded strange now, too. But also strangely . . . right.

She didn't have time to dwell on the absurdity of this notion because Ben had just ended his conversation and was swearing, long, low and imaginatively.

Folding her arms and leaning a shoulder against the doorjamb, Marcie decided it was a good thing she wasn't a prude. Still, there were several expletives that gave pause even to someone as urbane as she considered herself to be.

"Sorry," Ben finally muttered with a brief but abashed glance at her. "But that damned woman..."

"Trouble?" Marcie asked sweetly.

Scrubbing a hand over his perspiring face, Ben nodded. "Potentially, at least." He expelled a harsh breath. "That was Rosalie James. She is coming to the ranch. The thing is, she's a business associate..."

"Really." Business associate, my foot, Marcie thought.

"...but also a personal friend of mine, and the Hilliers. Her family's known most of mine forever."

"Oh." Just like that, Marcie was brought back to earth. Her hand flew to her mouth. "Oh my God."

"Exactly," Ben said grimly. His eyes, troubled, met Marcie's. "I couldn't turn her down—she's bringing some papers for me to look over, too—but her visit is going to be a severe test of our acting ability, I'm afraid. She knows me quite well. In fact, after Jane—"

With a curt gesture, he dismissed that.

But Marcie said, "You had a thing."

With another curt gesture, he dismissed that, too. "The point is, she knows me pretty well. It's going to be difficult convincing her you've been in my life this whole last year since I worked with her in Trenton and you were never seen or mentioned. Any ideas?"

"Hmm." Marcie concentrated. Ben was right, this was important. If the woman was a friend of the Hilliers, then everything that occurred during this visit was bound to be relayed to them.

It was therefore crucial that she and Ben convince their guest—and thus the Hilliers—that they had been lovers for quite some time. And, most importantly, that the child was Ben's.

"Did you travel in the course of your business?" she asked.

"Yes." Ben's head came up, a glimmer of comprehension dawning in his eyes. "Sure. I traveled regularly."

"Well, then, that's it," Marcie exclaimed triumphantly. "You had me stashed away in a love nest."

"You don't mind?" Ben asked. "After all, there was John...."

"Yes, but Rosemary doesn't know that. It's not like we're going to tell her who I really am. Right?"

"Right," Ben agreed reluctantly. Having decided to give Marcie his protection, he hated to think Rosalie's visit might jeopardize her in some way. "And it's Rosalie, not—"

"Whatever," Marcie said, her mind on part two of the plan. "And when she asks how far-gone I am, we'll say six months. That ought to muddy the waters some more, just in case...."

It was the next day. Rosalie James had arrived, introductions had been made and then Marcie had excused herself to lie down.

Predictably, the question, "And when is the happy event?" had been asked.

Their vague reply of "Sometime early in the New Year" had been accepted.

The question Marcie had been burning to ask was, "How long are you planning to stay?" But good manners had prevailed; the question had gone unuttered.

In its stead, another one presented itself to Marcie as she lay on her bed resting. One that neither she nor Ben had thought to address in the course of yesterday's planning session.

It had no sooner popped into her head and she was on her way to confront her husband.

"Kertin." After a cursory knock, Marcie stuck her head in the door of Ben's study. "I want to have a word with you."

"I was afraid of that." With a fatalistic sigh, Ben shifted his attention from his morose contemplation of the computer keyboard to Marcie's tight face. He had fled to his study at the first opportunity, made a few phone calls and sat down at the computer, thinking he would distract himself with some bookkeeping or something. He didn't want to dwell on the fact that he now had *two* unwanted women on his ranch.

But so far, his thoughts had been on anything but ranching business, and he had yet to turn the computer on.

Absently noting the hand Marcie was pressing into the small of her back and the dark circles beneath her—now sparking—brown eyes, he inquired without any real interest, "Where's our guest?"

"*Your* guest." Marcie closed the door and came all the way into the room. She perched on the arm of one of his deep chairs, not about to sit in the chair itself since she knew she'd never get out without Ben's help and a lot of awkward scrambling.

She already felt clumsy and ungainly enough—especially since Her Slender Litheness, Rosalie James, had made her entrance.

The woman was everything Marcie was not, even before the pregnancy—sleek sophistication from the tips of her Italian boots to the top of her smooth and stylish chignon. Add to that, designer clothes, understated jewelry and a smile that was an orthodontist's dream, and even a woman with an ego as relatively healthy as Marcie's couldn't help but be envious.

Envious, nothing. Marcie's hands were fairly itching to rearrange a few of Rosalie James's oh-so-perfect features.

"She's unpacking." The look Marcie shot Ben could have cut glass. "In *your* bedroom."

"You would have preferred I put her in *yours?*" Ben had sensed the tension and barely veiled animosity between the two women right from the start. At a loss as to its cause—he ruled out jealousy because, after all, he had been totally up-front with Rosalie about his "commitment" to Marcie, and Marcie barely even saw him as a friend—he had finally dismissed it as one of those women's things.

"Hmm?" he persisted, arching his brows when Marcie didn't answer right away.

She shot him a resentful glare. "No," she said, "but that does bring me to the point of my visit."

"I wondered what it was," Ben muttered, holding up his palms in a gesture of peace when Marcie sliced him another glare.

"Where were *you* planning to sleep now that Her Highness has got your bed?"

"Me?" Ben eyebrows arched higher. "Why, with you, of course. After all, we're—"

"But that's just it," Marcie heatedly interrupted, finally getting to the real heart of the thing that had her so bent out of shape: sharing a bed with Ben. "When I agreed to play the part of your devoted wife, I in no way intended that we should sleep together."

"Just what *had* you intended?" Ben asked, his interest piqued by Marcie's rather irrational behavior.

Land sakes, it wasn't as if he'd given her reason to fear for her virtue.

"Well, I don't know." Marcie, upset without really knowing why, refused to meet Ben's eyes. "I hadn't thought."

"That much is obvious," Ben said, feeling put-upon.

"I also didn't expect her to be so gorgeous," Marcie said so miserably that Ben was out from behind his desk and in front of her in one swift move.

"Whoa," he said softly. "What's this?"

Cupping Marcie's chin, he gently urged her face around till she looked at him. He searched her eyes. "Insecurities, from the indomitable Marcie Jacobs?"

"Hillier," she said in a choked voice.

"Kertin," Ben corrected.

Marcie's eyes clung to his. "For now," she said, blinking.

"For now," Ben agreed with such a surprisingly tender smile, Marcie's heart stopped.

She didn't know what was the matter with her, or why Rosalie James's relationship—whatever it was with Ben—should bother her so. But it did.

"You've slept with her," she accused, her eyes narrowing on Ben's, which were now, incredibly, alight with amusement.

She had wondered how he would look smiling a genuine smile. Well, now she knew. Devastatingly handsome, that's how.

Perversely, this made her resent him—and that woman—all the more. "Haven't you?" she prodded.

"No." Ben chuckled, unable to keep from being captivated by this vulnerable yet almost territorial side of Marcie, a side he had never imagined he'd see. "My contact with her has largely been business rather than personal. She is HK Industry's marketing vice president and as such, our so-called dates were, more often than not, working lunches, dinners or weekends."

"But you have kissed her."

"Well, I..." Ben let that go with an abbreviated shrug.

Which was more eloquent than a thousand words, Marcie thought, exclaiming, "*Aha!* You did kiss her. You cheater!"

"Cheater?" Ben repeated, nonplussed.

"Yes!" Marcie put her face close to his. "While I was tucked away in that love nest, growing fat with your child, you were out there wining, dining and *kissing* other women!"

"It wasn't like that," Ben laughingly protested, his eyes drawn to the freckles that were sprinkled across the bridge of Marcie's nose like raisins on a cinnamon bun.

His gaze moved to her lips, as inviting and puffy as a soft satin pillow. And to him, suddenly, incredibly sexy.

Without conscious intent, he leaned forward and covered them with his own. Marcie's startled gasp was swallowed. The hands she instinctively brought to his chest, became trapped there by one of his. His other hand slid into the soft jumble of curls at the back of her head, urging her closer.

Marcie complied, not so much from the slight pressure of his hand as in response to a sudden surge of unexpected need. She moaned as Ben took the kiss deeper, as exploration became bold possession.

One satiny stroke of tongue against tongue—that's all it took for passion to ignite. A passion of such force and magnitude, it stole Marcie's breath, stirred up a tempest in her blood and made her heartbeat thunder like a stampeding herd of Montana cattle.

Thoroughly frightened by her body's responses—not even John, when their love had been still young, had ever made her hunger like this—Marcie tensed. She was poised to struggle for release when a startled "Oops," followed by a slightly shrill and off-key feminine laugh abruptly caused Ben to draw back.

Their breathing labored, Ben's eyes betraying the same kind of shock and emotional turbulence as Marcie was feeling, they stared at each other for one pulsing moment while the aftershocks of passion still rocked them.

"So that's how that baby came to be," Rosalie quipped with another false laugh. "Have a care you don't hurt our little mother with those lusty appetites of yours, Benedict dear."

Her tone inferred she knew all about Benedict's appetites and that, together with her patronizing attitude, put Marcie's teeth on edge. Instead of pulling away from Ben as first intended, she leaned into him with a limpid smile.

"My Papa Bear could never hurt me," she purred, batting her lashes a bit as she gazed up at Ben adoringly. She puckered her lips. "Just one more kiss for Mama Bear and then she'll go take her nap."

"Behave yourself," Ben growled, but couldn't quite keep his lips from twitching any more than he could hang on to his chagrin over the conviction that he'd blown the lid off a hornet's nest of problems with his impulsive kiss. Papa Bear, indeed. He stifled a chuckle. "We're embarrassing our guest."

Mindful of his role as the smitten husband, he kept his arm around Marcie as he gave Rosalie a smile. "Are you all settled in? The room okay?"

"It's fine. A bit rustic, but—" Rosalie's eyes swept the study "—I suppose that's the, uh, charm of the wild West, isn't it."

She looked at Ben, somehow managing to give the impression that it was just the two of them, that Marcie had turned to thin air. "Not tired yet of playing farmer, my friend?"

"Oh, no," Marcie heartily preempted Ben's reply. She wasn't about to be dismissed by this alley cat in pedigree clothing. The nerve of the woman, to take such an intimate tone with a man who so clearly belonged to another.

"My Kertykins just loooves Montana." She kissed Ben's chin and sweetly smiled. "Don't you, Cup-cakes?"

"Watch it," Ben warned softly through a smile as fake as Marcie's. Grazing her lips with his own to keep up appearances, he just as softly added, "You're not too old to spank."

"Ooh," Marcie cooed, though in the wake of his light kiss it took a whole lot more effort to keep up the game. "I love it when you get mean. I hope you'll forgive us," she said to the visibly incensed Rosalie James, and inwardly cringing at the girlish giggle with which she laced her words. "We're just so darned crazy about each other."

Flirtatiously gazing into Ben's eyes and seeing them darken with something potently male, she caught her breath. Suddenly frantic because every one of those explosive emotions she had experienced during their kiss had sprung back to life, she slid off her perch on the armrest and distractedly glanced at her watch. "Heavens! Will you look at the time."

She rushed to the door. "You two have a drink while I see about dinner."

"Cookie's making supper." Ben's voice stopped her in the act of opening the door.

Reluctantly, she looked back at him across her shoulder. Damn, but she didn't want to play their game anymore. "But..."

"We'll be eating at six," Ben said. He got up and walked over to her. "That leaves a whole other hour for you to nap in."

He laid a hand on her shoulder. Marcie felt it like a brand. All too aware that something between them had shifted, and pretty damn sure she didn't like it, she had the strongest urge to duck out of his hold. And to bolt. But she didn't. She only stood there like a ninny while Ben said to Rosalie, "There's martini fixings in the sideboard. Why don't you go ahead and mix us a drink while I go tuck my..."

Marcie felt the pressure of his hand increase as he hesitated a fraction before saying, "...my little Marciekins into bed."

As Rosalie assented, they exited the room. When the door closed behind them, Marcie shrugged off Ben's hand. "Little Marciekins?" she hissed with a shudder. "I may throw up!"

"No worse than Kertykins." Ben herded her toward the bedroom. "You were laying it on pretty thick in there."

"Well, she asked for it." Becoming aware that she was being herded, Marcie belatedly balked. "Quit pushing me. And why this sudden need to see me tucked in?"

"We need to talk."

"We talked already." And she didn't like how that particular talk had ended. No, sir.

Ben reached past her, opened the bedroom door and ushered her through. "We weren't finished."

"Well, whose fault was that?" God, she wished she hadn't asked that. Because, just like that, they were looking at each other and it was all there again between them. The heat and the hunger.

But also their resentment of it.

"Mine, of course," Ben snapped, stalking to the window. The yard lights were on and he stared out at the bare branches of the cottonwoods over by the barn. The snow was all gone. Everyone was enjoying the small respite from winter, all the more so because they knew it would be short-lived. "It's always the man's fault, isn't it?"

"And what's that supposed to mean?" Because she needed to move, Marcie waddled to the bed and yanked back the spread.

"I hope you've got some more pillows," she griped, fiercely plumping the two that were there. "Because I'm not giving up one of mine."

Turning, Ben stared at her without comprehension. "Pillows?"

Marcie stared back. "Yes, pillows. To sleep on. To-night, when you . . ."

Their gazes locked and the words trailed away. Disconcerted, and impatient with it, Marcie swung her head to the side. She shoved both hands into her hair, then anchored them on top of her head as though trying to keep a lid on herself as she forced herself to look at Ben once again.

"This isn't going to work."

"What isn't? The marriage or our sleeping arrangement?" Though he spoke calmly, Ben was far from calm. More, he was convinced that Marcie was right. Things weren't going to work out as handily as he had thought in the immediate wake of Rosalie's unexpected phone call. A couple of days of pretense, he had thought. How difficult could that be?

Never in his wildest dreams would he have thought that a woman like Marcie, who wasn't even remotely his type and who was about as pregnant as it was possible for a woman to be, would have the power to do what many a more beautiful and alluring sophisticate had not been able to, namely to breach his formidable defenses and stir his juices.

Stir, hell. Ben's breath hitched on an inward chuckle-cum-groan. Marcie's response to his kiss had been at first so surprisingly shy and then so soul-stirringly sweet, it had whipped his blood into a frenzy. Just looking at her, he wanted it again.

Well, he was damned well not going to have it.

Grimly, though it was himself he was mad at, not her, Ben turned around and snapped down the blind, shutting out the halogen glare. "If my bunking down here with you is what's got you in a snit, you can relax. I've seen you in bed, remember?"

He turned to face her, his tone deliberately cold to douse the unwanted heat that flared between them.

"And I'm not so hard up that I'd get turned on by a near-term pregnant woman swathed in a nightgown by Omar the Tentmaker."

Chapter Five

To think she had let him kiss her! To think she had kissed him back! Or had it been the other way around?

Restless, grunting, Marcie shifted onto her side. But that wasn't comfortable, either. She flopped back into a prone position.

Either way, it had been a mistake, that kiss. And her reaction to it had been a disaster. Not to mention juvenile. A kiss, for crying out loud! What did it mean in the universal scheme of things? Nothing! Why, she couldn't even begin to count the number of kisses she had experienced in her time.

Omar the Tentmaker...

Damn him. A totally ridiculous urge to cry closed Marcie's throat. Proof that she was overtired, she told herself. Overtired and overpregnant.

She knocked against the taut drum of her stomach with her knuckles. "Hey, Widget," she called softly, the words a strangled mixture of chuckle and sob.

"This'd be a great time for you to make your entrance."

No matter that she was officially only six months pregnant right now, going into labor would solve everything. By the time she was back on her feet, Rosalie James would have split, the need for making like honeymooners would have been eliminated and she herself would be too busy tending to Widget to worry about hormones and Ben Kertin.

"Come on, Widget," she whispered, her voice cracking. And then, to her amazement, twin droplets of moisture welled out from beneath her closed lids and ran in stinging little rivulets into her ears.

Marcie's hands flew up to her face, her fingers touching the wetness there even as a harsh sob burst out of her throat like a cork from a bottle.

For the first time since forever, she cried.

The next day was a beaut. A hard frost had hit during the night and the day was clear and sunny.

Exhausted from her crying jag, Marcie had begged off from dinner when Ben had come to rouse her the previous night. In the wake of her tears had come a lassitude that had allowed her to sleep soundly the whole night through.

Ben had not come to share her bed.

In the shower, turning her face directly into the spray, Marcie told herself she was glad. And that if he had spent the night with Rosalie James, that was fine with her, too.

But somehow, in her heart of hearts, she *knew* Ben had not slept with the other woman.

She turned off the shower and, keeping her back to the full-length mirror on the bathroom door, briskly

toweled herself dry. She could hear male voices calling
something to each other out in the yard. Raucous
laughter followed. Someone must have told a joke. In
the far distance an engine of some kind sprang to life.

The grandfather clock in the living room chimed
once. Marcie figured that made it half past nine. She
couldn't remember the last time she had slept till nearly
nine in the morning. But, facing the mirror now that
she had on her roomy bathrobe, it was obvious by her
clear eyes and pink cheeks that the long rest had done
her good. Also, she was pleased to note, it had erased
all evidence of last night's tears.

After slipping into her customary sweats, she made
up the bed. She became aware with half a mind that the
house was awfully quiet. No radio sounds, no floors
creaking or doors shutting or any other of the multi-
tude of little noises that indicated someone was home.
There was no smell of coffee or of food.

Could it be that Ben and Whosit had gone out?

And why wouldn't they have? she immediately chal-
lenged herself, giving the decorative throw pillows a
couple of good punches for extra measure. In his role
of host to Ms. Hoity-Toity, Ben would naturally be
expected to show his guest around.

But what about our honeymoon?

Widget's swift kick followed right on the heels of
that inner whine, forcing a rueful chuckle out of
Marcie.

"Thanks," she murmured, and interrupted her
fussing with the already immaculate bed to rub her
hands lovingly over the mound of her stomach. "You
little lazybones. I wondered when you'd wake up but
now I know—just in time to tell your mom to get a
grip, right?

"Honeymoon..." With a self-deprecating snort, she rapped her knuckles against the side of her head. "Hello! Anybody home? There is no *honeymoon,* dum-dum. It's only pretend, remember?"

And a good thing, too, she silently added crossly, reminding herself that for all his moments of kindness, Ben Kertin was still a part of the Hillier family. And that if she were deluded enough to seek lasting security for her child—as well as more of Ben's dizzying kisses—by trying to make their marriage anything more than it was now, she would run the very real risk of having the very child she was trying to protect snatched from her arms forever.

Fiercely, she hugged her soon-to-be-born baby, bending her head as she vowed, "They'll never get you, Widget. Never. You're all I've got, and all that I'll ever need."

A sharp rap on the closed bedroom door made her start, effectively ending the moment of fervent communication. Before Marcie could form a response, the door swung wide to reveal Ben Kertin's imposing form.

Who else? Marcie groused.

"It's customary to wait for the words *Come in,*" she told him ungraciously. It bugged her that the sight of him—tall, broad and virile as all get-out—was suddenly able to make her heart turn over.

"And a good morning to you, too." Ben's eyes moved away from Marcie's face to rake her sweat-suited form. He didn't bother to disguise a grimace of distaste.

Noticing, Marcie's hostility doubled. But before she could give it voice, Ben spoke once again.

"Have you given any thought to making some changes in your wardrobe?"

"Frankly, no."

Once more, he looked her critically up and down. "Do you have *anything* besides John's castoffs?"

"Sure." She tossed her head. "I have those white sweats I wore the day of our wedding."

One corner of Ben's mouth twitched. Marcie knew by now that this constituted an abbreviated smile. "Comfortable as those sweats no doubt are," he murmured, walking all the way into the room until he stood in front of her, "they'll look terrible on our family pictures."

Too close, Marcie thought, and moved a step back. "What family pictures? There won't be any family pictures of you and me."

"Sure there will." Ben took another step, too. "Rosalie insists on doing the honors. She's appalled that we don't have wedding photos. She's quite the amateur photographer, you know."

"Oh, really?" Enveloped as she was by Ben's shower-clean scent and body heat, and aggravatingly disturbed by it, Marcie would have liked to take the necessary step to create some distance between them. But the bed was right behind her. The backs of her legs were flush against the side of the mattress. "Spent the night looking at her etchings, did you?"

Had she really said that? Oh, but she wished she hadn't said that! Especially when she saw Ben's smile deepen and some unsettling glints adding a rakish sparkle to his coal-black eyes.

"Photographs," he corrected, "not etchings." His tone had taken on an intimate quality that Marcie told herself was most annoying. As was the touch of his hand when he caught a curling tendril of her hair and rubbed it gently between thumb and forefinger. "I'm glad you're feeling more like yourself again this morning.''

Marcie swallowed against the constriction in her throat. It seemed to be a by-product of the tightness in her chest that was making it difficult to catch a breath. She tried to be angry, tried to think. Trust him to rub it in that I was crying.

But as she watched him raise the curl of hair to his nose and, with his eyes half closing, deeply inhale its just-washed fragrance, she couldn't rouse herself to animosity. She was too busy steeling herself against his potent appeal.

And when he laid his palm against the side of her face and with his thumb gently stroked across her eyebrow, it was all she could do not to turn into the caress like a kitten longing to be stroked.

"You had me worried," he said quietly, and the light in the eyes that held hers mesmerized darkened and softened with what could only be compassion and concern.

Or was it pity?

Marcie leapt at the chance to call it that and thus break the spell this man had for some reason chosen to weave. She jerked her face away from his touch, and glared at him. "So are my clothes an embarrassment in front of your snooty friend?"

Watching Ben's gaze turn oblique and his lips thin, Marcie felt like a shrew. Which promptly made her angrier. With him.

"I keep forgetting that people like you and the Hilliers equate outward appearance with character," she flung out. "Crummy clothes, crummy character, isn't that how it goes?"

Ben shook his head, frowning now. "Why are you doing this?"

Marcie sidled away from him. Feeling on the defensive, she pretended not to understand. "Doing what?"

"Lumping me in with John's parents. Picking a fight."

With a pseudocareless shrug, Marcie turned away. She went to the dresser and picked up the watch she had laid there last night. Her fingers shook as she tried to strap it onto her wrist.

"So where's Whatsername?" she tossed back in a brittle voice.

"You know perfectly well what her name is," Ben growled. And more moderately, added, "Roger is showing her the ranch. On horseback."

"Ah." Still unwilling to look at him, Marcie fussed with the odds and ends that littered the dresser. "Not only a photographer but an equestrienne, too."

"Marcie, what's bothering you?" Ben spoke quietly, from right behind her. Marcie's head came up, her eyes meeting his in the mirror. "And don't try to pretend it's Rosalie James."

No, Marcie inwardly conceded as her gaze once again helplessly tangled with Ben's. Rosalie James was not the cause of her depression and ire.

"Oh, I don't know." Letting her fisted hands drop to her sides, Marcie wrenched her gaze from Ben's and blindly stared toward the window. Blinking back the mortifying sting of tears, she latched on to the first, and least problematic, of her miseries. "I'm so damn sick of looking like the Goodyear blimp!"

"Aw, sweetheart . . ." Gently, Ben took her by the shoulders and turned her into his comforting embrace. "Come here. . . ."

To Marcie's total self-disgust, she immediately dissolved into what she considered blubbering foolishness.

"You said Omar the Tentmaker makes my nightieees," she wailed, pressing her face into his chest and soaking his wool flannel shirt. "A-and I d-don't have anything to w-wear f-for any stu-pid f-family photos, ei-theeerrr..."

"Shh, shh...yes, you do," Ben soothed, smoothing his large hand up and down Marcie's back with long, comforting strokes. "You will have, because that's what I came in here for..."

Leaning back a little, he caught Marcie's chin and tilted her tear-streaked face up to his. "...to take you shopping."

"Sh-shopping?" A little hiccup escaped her. "N-now?"

"Anytime you're ready."

"F-for a dress?"

"For anything you want." Ben's eyes twinkled, but something else, something soft and fuzzy warm that made Marcie feel oddly cherished and...and *understood,* lurked in their blackness, as well. "If you feel up to it."

"Well, I..." Sniffling, feeling self-conscious and a little giddy, Marcie wanted to say yes. She wanted to look, if not beautiful or even pretty, at least as good as she could.

The realization surprised her. It seemed like forever since she had cared about her appearance. As long as it was as bizarre as possible, she had been content.

The shrink she had once spent a few sessions with had asked her why she thought that was. Clearly, he had wanted her to admit that her outlandish outfits, her lavish makeup and rainbow palette of hair colors served as a disguise of some sort, a facade behind which she hid her true self.

Horse apples, had been her opinion, and that had been the end of therapy. After which she had dressed and behaved crazier than ever. It had been an expression of her artistic self, of her individuality. A bid to be noticed, she supposed, as a free spirit and something of a revolutionary.

When had it gotten old?

Somewhere around the time of John's death. Or, more accurately, on discovering that she was going to be a mother. Somehow she had come to feel then that this new status—motherhood—required her to settle down, to adopt a more . . . conventional demeanor.

Even still, this amazed her. Shades of, You can take a girl out of middle-class, but you can't take the middle-class out of the girl? How truly trite. And yet . . . amazing. And funny.

Funny, because this craving for respectability had hit her when she was too poor to do anything about it except to pretend it didn't exist.

But now, here was her chance to at least get a dress. A nice dress. Perhaps even an elegant one. Visions of herself in something soft and clinging rose before her eyes. . . .

And then she looked down, caught sight of her medicine ball of a stomach, and her shoulders slumped.

"By any chance," she whispered dejectedly, "does this tentmaker of yours have a local salon?"

While Rosalie was still off on horseback somewhere, Ben drove Marcie to the town of Curtis, some thirty miles east of Deer Falls. It had several smart boutiques, and in one of them they found an ensemble the dress of which was of a high-waisted Empire-style that would be flattering even after the baby's birth. The color of a sapling ponderosa pine, it was made of a smooth, butter-soft, winter-weight rayon that draped Marcie's body like the finest silk but without clinging where it shouldn't. The accompanying jacket was a relaxed cut blazer with just enough additional flair to make it something special.

The price tag made Marcie hurriedly try to hang the outfit back on the rack, but Ben insisted she at least try it on.

It was perfect. Hardly recognizing herself, Marcie emerged somewhat reluctantly from the dressing room to model it for Ben. While looking her up and down, something wild flared in his dark eyes and Marcie's heart tripped over itself the way it had been prone to do with alarming regularity of late.

But then Ben scowled, more fiercely than Marcie had ever seen him, and brusquely turned away.

Interpreting his forbidding expression as displeasure, Marcie quickly said, "I know, it's too expensive. I'll go take it off."

"Only to have it wrapped," he shocked her by growling. "Unless you don't like it?"

"Oh, I do, but—"

At her uncertain tone, his eyes snapped to her face. Seeing the worry there, he bit off an oath. When would he learn to moderate his reactions around her? he asked himself angrily. Wasn't her emotional state precarious enough without his moods?

"I'm a jerk," he said with a sigh and a crooked little smile. He raised his hand as if to touch her, but dropped it as he thought better of it. Touching her proved to be dangerous these days. Dangerous because it was addictive. "You look . . . beautiful."

Marcie couldn't help it—for a moment she just stood there with what she was sure was a dopey grin on her face.

"Thank you, Ben," she whispered, and didn't even mind when he scowled at her with an impatient wave of the hand.

"Anything else you want?" he all but snapped.

"No." Marcie shook her head. The dress, and his compliment, were more of a gift than she would ever have expected of him.

But they did end up buying her some shoes, as well as some frills and accessories Ben insisted she had to have. He would have bought her a winter coat, too, but Marcie refused to try anything else on as long as she was big as a house.

Because Ben was suddenly in a hurry, they grabbed a fast-food lunch on the run, after which they made their way back to the ranch.

Ben was morose and silent, replying in curt monosyllables to Marcie's attempts at conversation. Eventually, in disgust, she gave up trying and tuned the radio to a country-and-western station, leaving Ben to his thoughts.

They were dark ones. Troubled ones. And they had to do with the fact that he had come to enjoy way too much the company of the woman in the passenger seat. It was becoming much too easy to be with her, and much too difficult to remember she was only passing through.

And that he wanted it that way.

At the ranch, Rosalie, an equestrian vision in cream-colored jodhpurs, blue denim shirt and down vest, smilingly welcomed them back.

Marcie immediately developed a headache and withdrew to her room. She didn't emerge again until it was time for predinner drinks in the living room, and would have avoided that, too, if Ben hadn't rather coolly informed her that he expected her to make a hostess's effort.

Sipping her mineral water while the other two drank wine, Marcie was doing her best to be vivacious. In her new dress, with her hair somewhat sleek and her makeup carefully understated, she felt reasonably able to hold her own against the other woman's exquisite wardrobe and grooming.

She smiled sweetly for Rosalie's camera, and did her utmost to participate in the conversation. The latter proved an uphill battle, since Rosalie seemed determined to exclude her from it.

All through Cookie's excellent roast beef dinner and the hot apple pie dessert, she and Ben went on and on about mergers and stock options and capital investments, making Marcie not only feel like an ignoramus, but boring her into a near coma, as well.

By the end of the meal, Marcie was fuming. She would have loved to give *her* husband as well as his arrogant guest a piece of her mind, but wisely resisted. *She* would have been the one who looked the fool, she decided, and made a point of imitating Ben's withdrawn demeanor instead.

Declining his invitation for coffee and brandy in his study since she could partake of neither and had had all she could take on the subject of business and high finance, she pleaded exhaustion and went back to her room.

Neither Ben nor Rosalie offered even a token protest.

Ben's "I'll see you later" had been curt.

Now, lying in bed, she tried to read but couldn't keep her mind on the fast-paced thriller any more than she'd been able to follow the dinner conversation. Her thoughts kept veering to Ben.

He had been so sweet to her that morning—taking her shopping and all. And then, pow—just like that he had turned remote, even cold, again for the rest of the day.

Was it that he regretted spending all that money on her? Did he think she was a money-grubbing gold digger for accepting his purchases? Had taking her shopping been some kind of a test? One she had failed?

Oh, hell!

"Widget, I'm about to lose my bloody mind!" Fed up to the teeth with the games her mind insisted on playing, she tossed the book aside. She struggled over onto her side. Uncomfortable, she punched some pillows.

Even the extra ones that hadn't been there earlier in the day.

"I guess that means His Lordship is planning on sharing this bed," she groused aloud as she wriggled and punched. "In which case, I just wish he'd hurry up and get here. This waiting is driving me— Oh. Hi."

Up on one elbow, Marcie forced a sickly smile as Ben strode into the room.

"Hi." Already loosening his tie, he barely spared her a glance. His expression was dark.

Marcie's heart sank. "Long day, huh?"

"Hmm." His jacket followed the tie he had tossed over the back of a chair. Half-turned away, Ben briskly undid his cuffs, untucked the shirt and unbuttoned the front, all with the sort of short, jerky movements that bespoke a barely leashed temper. Or anger.

Oh, boy, Marcie thought, completely convinced now that she was the source of his displeasure.

What she had no way of knowing, of course, was that Ben's scowl had been caused by nothing more sinister than an intense case of the jitters with regard to their sleeping arrangement.

It didn't matter that he knew there wouldn't be any hanky-panky. What bothered the hell out of him was that he wished . . .

No, dammit, he wasn't even going to think it.

His motions rough with suppressed tension, Ben jerked off the shirt and wadded it, whirling around when from behind him he heard Marcie gasp.

"You all right?" he demanded.

Swallowing, her eyes saucer-sized and riveted on Ben's truly magnificent torso, Marcie nodded. "For a pencil pusher," she blurted without thinking, "you sure are *built*."

Staring at her, nonplussed, Ben noted the precise instant when it hit her what she had said. If possible, her eyes grew wider still, and she swung them up to his face. A helpless sort of titter escaped her and she clapped a hand over her mouth.

For the length of one heartbeat, Ben was too captivated by her wide eyes and flushed cheeks to react. But then, to Marcie's shock and surprise, a shout of laughter burst from him.

He tossed the wadded shirt, football fashion, into the nearest corner, strode to the bed and, dropping down on the edge of the mattress, caught Marcie by the shoulders and hauled her into his arms for a fierce hug.

"Man, but you're something," he growled as laughter fled and he pressed his cheek against her hair.

"Yeah, but what?" Marcie quipped, though it took an effort to get the words past the boulder that had lodged itself in her throat. And it wasn't Ben's nearness that was choking her up, though the feel of his hot, hard and hair-roughened chest against her cheek had shoved her heart rate into overdrive.

No, the thing that made her throat ache and her eyes sting was the surge of protective tenderness that welled up inside her. It was as startling as it was overwhelming. And what had caused it was the expression on Ben's face that had followed her impulsive observation. An expression that had been a mixture of surprise, vulnerability and an almost childlike longing that was completely at odds with everything she had thought she knew about the Iron Man.

The Iron Man. That was the tag she had privately hung on him, and not as a compliment. On short acquaintance, she had thought him rigid and unfeeling, chauvinistic and arrogant.

But in that brief instant a couple of moments ago, when he'd looked at her unguarded, she had become convinced that, deep down, Ben Kertin was none of those things. More, that the forbidding, even cold, facade he presented to the world was strictly that: a facade. A wall behind which hid a very sensitive man, one who had known more than his share of pain.

And who understood a woman's need for a pretty dress.

Feeling as though she wanted to spare him from ever being hurt again, but only too aware that Ben would not welcome the knowledge that she'd seen past his defenses, Marcie slipped her arms around his lean middle and briefly hugged him back.

Pulling back, she gave him a cocky grin. "You feel as good as you look," she said. "What did you do, pump iron?"

"Nuh-uh." While Ben loosened his embrace, he did not release her. "I used to run."

"From your creditors or from the IRS?"

"Neither." Grinning back at her, he flicked the tip of her nose. "You're a brat, you know that?"

"So that's what you meant when you said I was something."

"No." Ben's grin faded. His eyes lost their teasing glint and became intense. "That's not what I meant. And you know it.

"Don't you?" he prompted, his arms tightening around her when Marcie, too, lost her grin and just mutely gazed up at him.

Ben felt as though he could lose himself in the shimmering brown pools of her eyes. "Answer me," he whispered, his voice husky with emotions he hadn't allowed himself to feel since Kirby and Jane.

Emotions he still wasn't at all sure he liked for this woman to make him feel, either.

Protectiveness. Indulgence. Tenderness. Somehow, when he wasn't looking, they kept sneaking up on him.

"Yes," Marcie said, and the softness of her expression eased something twisted and cramped within Ben's breast.

He tugged her against him and lowered his head— only to earn himself a kick of such unexpected magnitude, he jerked back with a startled "What the—?"

Marcie, with an apologetic chuckle, fell back against the pillow. Inwardly, she blessed Widget's timing since, to her, the situation had threatened to become unsettlingly intimate. The covers had slid down so that they were bunched at the top of her thighs. Other than the daisy pattern of her flannel nightie, there was nothing to obstruct Ben's view of Widget's kick-boxing demonstration.

"I need to have a word with that kid," he murmured with mock gruffness, though something told him he had just been saved from acting foolishly.

There had already been too damned much kissing going on between him and his...*wife*. And before them stretched the hours of the night. A night that would seem all the longer because he would be spending it with her. In bed.

Abruptly he stood. "I think I'll grab a shower."

The bathroom door across the hall fell shut behind him. Marcie twisted her head around to stare at it through the open bedroom door. She was thinking that she, too, would benefit from a dousing of water. Cold water. Lord, but that man could turn her on.

She squirmed restlessly, her ears straining toward the bathroom. But only the sound of rushing water could be heard. Apparently Ben was not a shower singer or whistler. Or maybe he just didn't feel like it tonight. She knew she wouldn't....

So, did he have pajamas in there?

The thought came at Marcie out of left field. She stiffened. Even more so when the bathroom door opened, disgorging a cloud of steam.

And Ben. Naked.

Chapter Six

Naked except for the towel around his hips.

Thank goodness. Marcie briefly closed her eyes, telling herself it was relief, not disappointment, that was causing the flutters in her stomach. Or maybe it was Widget, stroking her for once instead of kicking.

"Sorry," Ben murmured, not sure what to make of Marcie's expression. Was he embarrassing her, standing here in nothing but a towel? Surely not. After all, she had been married. Surely she had seen John wearing less, lots of times.

For some reason that thought didn't sit well. Gruffly he asked, "When you moved my stuff down from upstairs, where'd you put the pajamas?"

"Um." Clearing her throat and trying not to be obvious about her awestruck inspection of him, Marcie pulled the covers up to her chin. As though that would leave *him* any the less exposed. "In the, um, bottom drawer of the, uh, highboy."

With his back to her as he walked to the tall chest of drawers, Marcie was free to drink in the sight of his powerful body. And here she had thought John had been a hunk...! Ha!

Broad of shoulder and lean of hip, in a Cosmo centerfold contest, Ben Kertin would have beat out his younger cousin hands down.

Or should that be *pants* down? Marcie thought naughtily, and giggled.

Hearing the smothered sound, Ben snapped upright and around. He was feeling more self-conscious than he'd felt since his first communal shower back in his high school football days. His towel came loose and he clutched it.

"What?" he barked.

He glared so ferociously while struggling to keep the towel from coming undone that Marcie laughed all the harder. She helplessly shook her head, gasping for breath, only too aware that she was probably mere seconds away from full-fledged hysteria. It had been an emotionally trying day.

The slam of the bathroom door behind Ben snapped her out of it. Or, at least, it stopped her foolish laughter. It did nothing at all for the irrational tears that took its place.

With a sob that seemed to rise up all the way from her toes, she flopped onto her side and buried her face in her hands.

"Oh, John," she whispered brokenly, "what am I doing here? Why did you do this to me? Leave me like this? Why?"

"I used to ask Jane the very same thing."

Marcie hadn't heard Ben come out of the bathroom, hadn't felt the mattress dip as he climbed into bed next to her. He didn't touch her. Nor could Marcie have stood that just then. As though he knew it, he kept well away from her, on the far side of her.

But his voice reached out like a comforting caress, though it vibrated with an anguish Marcie understood only too well.

"I used to raise my arms and shake my fists," he said. "I used to prowl the night and howl at the moon. What had I done, I used to ask, that I deserved to lose every single person I ever loved?"

Listening, Marcie's sobs quieted. Her sorrow didn't lessen, on the contrary, it now grew to include some of Ben's. But she took comfort in knowing she was not the only one who had lost. It helped to be reminded of that.

"My parents died when I was eight," Ben said. Flat on his back, with his crossed arms pillowing his head, he stared up at the shadowed ceiling and saw himself as he had been at that age—knock-kneed and skinny in his first suit with long pants, seated beside Grandpa Hillier and Aunt Meg in that tiny memorial chapel with the stained-glass windows.

To this day he had an aversion to stained-glass windows.

"My parents died, too," Marcie confided in a halting whisper. "An avalanche in the Andes. I was fifteen."

"I'm sorry." Ben rolled his head to the side. He could barely make out the shape of Marcie's face. "Fifteen's a hard age to lose parents."

"There is no good age for something like that." Marcie swallowed, remembering just how hard it had been. "Is there?"

"No. I don't suppose there is."

"Want to tell me what happened?"

"Sure." Ben shifted his gaze once again to the ceiling. "It was an airplane crash. My mother was an impassioned aviatrix. In this day and age, I'm sure she would have been been the captain of the Concorde, or something. In her time, when she was younger, she crop dusted here in Montana. And after marrying Dad, which to the Hilliers other than Grandpa was the worst kind of lapse in good judgment, she only got to fly every once in a while. Whenever she and Dad, who was a struggling building contractor, could afford to rent a small plane. It was one of those rentals that killed them."

"How?" Marcie asked when Ben fell silent. She shifted awkwardly until she lay on her other side, facing him. She was glad that he had clicked off the bedside lamp when he'd come to bed. The pale light of the moon that illuminated the room seemed perfectly suited to their present mood of somber reflection.

"Nobody knows." Marcie dimly perceived Ben's slight shake of the head. "Years later I was told that they went down over the Cascades somewhere. That they just sort of dropped off the radar screen. They were never found."

"Oh, Ben, I'm sorry." Impulsively, Marcie reached out to him. Her eyes had gotten used to the semidarkness. Against the relative brightness of the moon, his profile was as sharply defined as a scissor cutting.

"Neither were my parents." Marcie swallowed another aching knot of tears. "And neither was John. Do you think...?"

She hesitated.

"What?" Ben shifted onto his side so that they lay facing each other. "Do I think what?"

Marcie gave a quick shake of the head, something Ben heard and felt rather than saw. "I wondered...would it have been any easier if we'd had bodies to bury? A grave to bring flowers to once in a while?"

"No." He said it curtly, roughly.

Too late Marcie remembered his wife and son. Heartsore with regret, she listened to him taking deep breaths. She didn't dare speak.

"No," Ben finally said again, and the sadness in his voice nearly broke Marcie's heart. "Sometimes I think it's harder. More final. Without that grave you can pretend, delude yourself they're still alive. With my son...I can't...."

The sentence faded, incomplete, into a ragged sigh and then, silence. Only the scratch of a branch against the window and the sound of their halting breaths could be heard.

"Oh, Ben," Marcie finally managed. "I'm so sorry."

"Yeah." All the bleakness of an anguished soul in one short syllable.

Wearily, Marcie closed her eyes. Perhaps they were better off trying to sleep.

But once started, Ben found it impossible not to keep talking.

"Death," he spat in a harsh whisper. "What makes it so hard to say that word? Why is it so much easier to say he passed away, or he was taken, or that he went home, when the truth is, he died. Period. He's dead. Kirby is dead."

His breath hitched. "And so is...his mother."

Rolling onto his back, he covered his eyes with his arm. "I loved them," he whispered in a strangled voice that twisted Marcie's gut into knots of helpless sympathy.

"When she...betrayed me, when they...died, a part of me—the good part, the part that cared about things and about...people—died, too."

"No, it didn't." Till then Marcie had not dared to move, hardly even to breathe. She knew instinctively that Ben had never talked this way with anyone, but that the need to unburden himself had weighed on him, had nearly crushed him, all these months.

His grief had needed to be shared, just as hers had needed to be. The difference was, she had had someone who had listened. Widget. Her baby. Talking to that small life and drawing comfort from its presence had made all the difference in the world.

How lucky she was! Marcie's hand strayed to her stomach where Widget had settled down for a nap.

And how truly deserving of sympathy was Ben who had convinced himself he had lost the ability to care, yet who had shown her in so many ways that he could indeed care, very much.

Compelled to show him that she did, too, Marcie raised up on one elbow and smoothed her free hand over his hair. It was still slightly damp from his shower, and lay full and sleek against his scalp.

"No, it didn't," she repeated in a whisper that was husky with emotion. "And who should know that better than I?"

With a groan, Ben turned to her, reached for her. "Let me hold you," he rasped. "Please, Marcie, just for tonight let me hold you."

Ben awoke to murky daylight and with a flannel-draped rump intimately nestled, spoon fashion, against his loins. There was just an instant of disorientation and then he knew. Marcie.

The events of the previous day, culminating with that—for him, totally out-of-character—baring of the soul, came back to him in a rush. Mortification scalded his cheeks. He closed his eyes and stifled an oath. His muscles tensed. He had to get out of here before she woke up.

Carefully, holding his breath, Ben eased away from the cozy warmth of human contact. He tamped down the sense of loss, ruthlessly telling himself that the last thing he wanted was this kind of intimacy.

Aside from the fact that neither he nor Marcie were in the market for a relationship that included shared sleeping arrangements, he never again wanted to put himself into the kind of position where he would *need* someone the way he had once needed Jane.

Need like that, love like that, made a man vulnerable. Left him wide open to pain. Only a masochist willingly asked to be hurt.

Grimly, Ben slipped off the bed. Ben Kertin was no masochist.

He tiptoed past the foot of the bed toward the bathroom. A floorboard creaked. He froze, snapping a glance toward the bed. And found himself trapped by a pair of wide-open, chocolate-colored eyes.

"Hi," Marcie said, and her heart ached in response to the remote expression that followed Ben's brief look of surprise and chagrin. The walls were up again, she realized. No doubt about it. After the closeness they had shared, the realization not only disappointed her, it made her mad.

"Running?" she asked quietly, keeping her gaze levelly fixed on his.

Ben didn't miss the sparks in her eyes, however. Nor the suppressed anger vibrating in her voice. Women, he thought with deliberate deprecation. Give 'em an inch and they think you owe them the whole damn mile.

"Hardly," he said in a clipped tone. "Seems to me I was making my way quite slowly toward the bathroom."

"On your tippy toes."

"I was trying not to wake you. Common courtesy, I'd say."

"Either that," Marcie called, raising up on an elbow when Ben abruptly terminated the exchange by stalking out of the room, "or yellow-bellied cowardice."

Reaching for the doorknob, Ben sent her a scathing glare and firmly shut the door.

Thump. Something bounced off it on the bedroom side.

Ben raised a brow, thinking, Damned if the little firebrand hadn't tossed a pillow after him!

Stepping into the bathroom, a smile tugged at one corner of his mouth. Catching a glimpse of himself in the mirror, however, it quickly faded. And he thought, She's right, you know. You are a coward.

And he didn't like himself very much.

They had managed to get themselves showered and dressed for the day without tripping over each other more than once or twice. Conversation had been confined to mumbled "Excuse me's" and "Pardon's."

Ben had beaten it out of the bedroom as quickly as he could, wearing jeans and a plaid Western-cut woolen shirt with the cuffs rolled up over a long-sleeved thermal undershirt.

With his Stetson on his head, he looked enough like the Marlboro Man to make Marcie's throat go dry, a fact that had her slamming closet doors and dresser drawers for quite some time after he had exited the room.

Damned macho jerk, she fumed. Would it kill him to unbend just a little? Just to show her she hadn't *dreamed* the moments of closeness last night? *Slam. Bang.*

What was he afraid of, anyway? That she'd try to lord it over him this morning? That she'd blab to one and all that Ben Kertin was human and susceptible to pain?

Moron! The closet door slammed shut with a satisfying *thunk*. Did he imagine the world would think less of him if it knew he missed and mourned his wife and son?

Or... Marcie sank down at the edge of the bed and thoughtfully stared at the thick woollen socks in her hand. Or could it be that this show of aloofness was simply a lonely man's way of coping with some nebulous guilt and bewilderment over the fact that the people he cared about... died? Meaning, it was better not to care. And in the event that you did care, pretend you didn't?

Awkwardly, her lips thoughtfully pursed, Marcie bent to the task of pulling on her socks.

"Good morning."

Walking into the kitchen, the first thing Marcie saw was Ben, Stetsonless, sitting with his head solicitously bent to Rosalie's as the latter held forth across a cup of coffee.

No doubt expounding on the advantages of mutual funds versus money market, Marcie inwardly sneered on her way to the stove and a much-needed cup of coffee.

Fascinating stuff, she thought, forcing a smile for Cookie who was hovering over the grill, pancake batter at the ready. Too fascinating, obviously, for either of them to return a civil greeting.

But just as that gripe had taken shape, Ben bounced to his feet and, suddenly all smiles, rushed to sweep Marcie into an embrace. "Good morning, sweetheart."

His kiss on the mouth could have caused a polar meltdown. "We've been waiting for you."

"Y-you have?" It was all Marcie could do not to spill the coffee she was holding, stiff-armed, as far from her body—and Ben's—as possible. "Am I, uh, late?"

"No." He kissed her nose, his expression as he peered into her face, all tenderness and care. His voice dropped, taking on an intimate timbre that would have curled Marcie's toes if not for the fact that she knew he was merely putting on a show for their audience. "Sleep well, my love?"

"Hmm." She sighed, striving to look suitably dreamy, but inwardly longing with all her heart to tromp on his foot. "How could I not, my sweet, after the way you— Oops! Do excuse us...."

She swept a look of apology toward Rosalie who was watching them with narrowed eyes. "I've been trying to tell this man that I'm too far-gone for...you know."

Batting her lashes, she sweetly smiled up at Ben. "But what can I say? He loves me. *Grrrr*," she growled and, going up on her toes, nipped at Ben's chin. "You tiger, you...."

"You're overacting," he murmured against her mouth.

"You started it," she replied the same way. For all the world, just two newlyweds whispering sweet nothings.

"Can we stop now?"

"I wish we would." She gave him a lingering kiss that felt a heck of a lot better than it had any business feeling.

Cookie sharply *harrumphed*. "If you folks'd just sit yerselves down," he groused, "mebbe I could get on wi' the rest of m' chores."

"Rosalie is leaving us this morning," Ben announced a short while later over stacks of delicious flapjacks. Cookie, satisfied that everyone had been adequately provided for, had returned to his own bailiwick, the cookhouse.

"Really." Marcie tried, unsuccessfully, to muster some genuine regret. "It was good of you to—"

"Don't bother with the niceties," Rosalie interrupted. She put down her knife and fork and dabbed at her lips with her napkin. "I don't believe we're fated to be friends. Do you?"

"Hmm." Marcie arched a brow, slanting a glance toward Ben who suddenly seemed absorbed in the task of swirling the coffee in his cup. She looked back at Rosalie with a cool smile. "Probably not."

Rosalie pushed back her chair. "If you want to bring the truck around, Benedict, I'm ready to go."

"Sure." With obvious relief, Ben got up from the table, grabbed up his hat and jacket and exited the room.

"I know I should wish you well," Rosalie said, standing model-straight and stylish next to her chair.

"But you won't," Marcie finished, still smiling. She was thinking that she had to hand it to the other woman—at least she was no hypocrite. She found that she liked her for that. Her smile warmed and she, too, tossed down her napkin and pushed herself to her feet. "That's okay. I understand."

"You're all wrong for him, you know," Rosalie said. Marcie nodded. "I know."

"He's a businessman. Together, he and I could have built an empire."

"If empire building were what he was after," Marcie said softly. "I don't believe he is, though. Not anymore."

"Thanks to you," Rosalie said bitterly.

But Marcie shook her head. "Much as I'd like to, I can't take the credit."

"You make it sound as if this—" Rosalie made a contemptuous sweep with her arm "—were an improvement on his former life."

"Yes. I think it is. Or, at least," Marcie qualified after a moment's thought, "it could be. With time."

"And *your* help?"

"Maybe." Marcie placed her hands against her stomach. "Mine and the baby's."

Only to herself did she add, *At least for a little while.*

By the time Ben returned from driving Rosalie to Missoula's Johnson-Bell Airport, Marcie had moved his belongings back upstairs, changed the sheets of both his bed and hers, baked a dried-apple pie and made a pot of spaghetti sauce from scratch, using Cookie's home-canned tomatoes.

"I haven't felt this energetic in weeks," she cheerfully announced when Ben found her in the guesthouse, scrubbing down kitchen walls. "And as you yourself once pointed out to me, here in *this* cottage is where I belong. With luck, I'll have the place habitable before Widget makes her entrance."

Ben scowled at her. Much as what she said was true—he *had* wanted her out of the main house—that had been then. Before... Well, before.

What had Rosalie said to him in the truck? "That little bride of yours seems to think that her charms and this ranch are sufficient to keep you content here in the back of beyond. Is she right?"

Ben had made no reply. He had changed the subject by asking some innocuous question of his own and Rosalie had been sensitive enough to get the message. Namely that his private thoughts and feelings were as off-limits for discussion now as they had ever been.

This didn't mean, however, that the question hadn't given him pause. It had. Especially since the startling answer to it seemed to be a resounding *yes*.

He had come to the Lazy H prepared to go it alone, had even looked forward to it. He had been annoyed, to say the least, to find that Marcie Jacobs—Hillier— had robbed him of the solitude he craved.

So when, exactly, had he stopped craving that solitude? At what point had Marcie's presence stopped being a thorn in his hide? How, and when in the short time they had lived under one roof, had she come to seem like a fixture in his life, a part of his routine that was as comfortable as an old bathrobe, as companionable as Rupert the hound dog had been in his youth? And, at the same time, as refreshing and exhilarating as a thunderstorm on a hot summer day?

Ben didn't know but, dammit, he did know he didn't want her moving out of his house. "What's your hurry, all of a sudden?" he growled.

Shrugging, Marcie blew a curl out of her eyes and stepped back to inspect the streaky result of her labors so far.

"Afraid I'll sneak into your bedroom at night, now that I've had a taste of sharing your bed?"

Marcie's answer was a mute rolling of the eyes in his direction. She was determined not to let him spoil her inexplicably happy mood. She had no idea where this good feeling had come from, though she was honest enough to admit Rosalie's departure had *something* to do with it. But it was more than that. She was filled with a giddy sort of expectancy—and it had somehow translated itself into an almost feverish need to build a nest.

In any case, she was having too much fun to question it and feeling too damn good to fight with Ben Kertin.

"This'll need painting, after all," she observed, her attention once again focused on the wall.

"Not by you, it won't."

"Well, of course by me." Marcie took up the sponge and began washing again. "Aside from the fact that I love to paint, there's really no one else to do it for me."

"When the time is right, there will be," Ben said shortly.

"And when will the time be right?" Marcie asked archly. "When *you* say so?"

"Damn straight when I say so," Ben growled. "Since I happen to be the boss."

"Of the ranch, not of me."

"This house is part of the ranch."

"But you said—" Marcie dropped the sponge into the pail and turned, arms akimbo. "Darn it, we have an agreement that says this house is mine."

"I'm aware of our agreement and I know what I said," Ben said curtly. "I've changed my mind."

For several long seconds of silence, he endeavored to stare her down. And then he added, "For as long as you stay at the ranch, I want you to live in the main house. With me."

Marcie could see that it had cost him to say that. She knew the kind thing to do would be to nod and say, Fine. I'll stay.

But she also knew this wasn't the time for kindness. It was a time for honesty. For openness. For mutual understanding of an *ongoing* nature. She didn't want the kind of yo-yoing, on-again-off-again friendship, for lack of a better word, of last night and this morning. She couldn't handle that. She hated the kind of tension and uncertainty it created.

And so she asked, "Why?"

"What do you mean, why?" Ben used anger as the rod with which to deflect Marcie's attempt to dig beneath the surface. "I married you and I'm inviting you to stay in my house. Isn't that good enough?"

"No, it's not good enough!" Marcie flared. Agitated, she paced. "If it's because of appearances, or because you can't think of a way to tell Cookie and Roger Stevens that we don't have a real marriage..."

"That is *not* the reason."

Marcie whirled. "Then tell me what is, for crying out loud!"

She watched Ben saunter into the small room, filling it with his presence. He cut a commanding figure, standing with his head high, legs slightly spread, the breadth of his shoulders emphasized by a bulky down vest. His profile, as he stared out the window with lowered brows, was brooding.

"I don't know," he said hoarsely.

Suddenly out of steam, Marcie sank down onto a dusty chair. "Not good enough, Kertin," she said.

"Then what the *hell* do you want?" Ben practically shouted, turning on her with an anguished expression that tore at her heart. "That I spill my guts, compromise my manhood, hand you something else you can pity me for?"

"Pity!" Marcie was on her feet, hands on her hips. "Is that what you think last night was all about?"

Shutters dropped, blanking out Ben's expression. "I don't want to talk about it."

"Well, *I* do!"

"Tough." He strode past her to the door.

"Ben!"

He hesitated, but didn't turn around. "What?"

"You walk out and I leave."

He did turn then, slowly. "No, you won't."

"Watch me."

"You've got nowhere to go."

"There's always somewhere to go." She walked toward him, slowly. "I might not like where it is, but it'll beat staying here unless..."

She deliberately let the sentence hang and, only a foot or so away from him, stopped walking. She gazed up at him, silently challenging him to ask the logical question.

After a moment of mutually somber contemplation, he did. "Unless what?"

"Unless you're willing to be friends."

He blinked, surprised, then gave a half-frowning laugh. "Well, if that's all," he said with a slight, uncomprehending shake of his head, "what's the big deal? We're friends already, aren't we?"

"Are we?" Marcie held his gaze, searched his heart. "Are we really?"

Ben's frown deepened.

"Friendship is a two-way street," she told him quietly.

"I know that."

"Friends trust one another."

"I'm aware of that, too."

"Trusting one another means we can make ourselves vulnerable without shrinking back in the light of day."

"You're talking about this morning."

"Yes," Marcie said quietly. "I'm talking about this morning. You acted as if last night had never been. How do you think that made me feel?"

"How?" As he asked, Ben raised a hand and gently wiped a smudge of dust off Marcie's cheek. "How did it make you feel?"

"Betrayed."

Marcie nodded in response to Ben's puzzled arching of brows. Her voice thickened as emotion tightened her throat. "You gave me a gift last night," she said, her voice rough with the remembered disillusionment of this morning, "the gift of trust, by telling me things that I somehow knew you hadn't talked about before.''

"I hadn't," Ben injected quietly.

"It made me feel . . . pride. Not *pity*," she said in a fierce aside. "I felt proud and grateful because you lowered your defenses and put aside your inhibitions to give me a glimpse of your own anguish in order to lessen mine. It gave me such comfort. And I thought . . ."

Marcie hesitated, drawing a deep breath and pressing her hands to her abdomen because, for just a moment there, she'd felt as if the bottom had dropped out of it.

"I thought," she continued when the sensation ceased almost as soon as it had begun, "that it gave you comfort, too."

"It did." Ben's hands were on Marcie's shoulders now, his thumbs moving back and forth across her collarbone in soothing, sensitizing strokes.

Marcie tipped back her head to search his eyes. "Then why?" she asked. "Why the cold shoulder this morning?"

"Because . . ." Ben took a deep breath. Faced with the caring concern and intensity of her expression, he knew only the truth would do.

"Because," he said, "it's just like you said. I'm a coward. A no-good, yellow-bellied—"

"No, you're not." Laughing—all the good feelings from before restored to her as if by magic—Marcie rose up on her toes and silenced him with a light kiss on the mouth. "You're—"

—*none of those things,* she had started to say when, suddenly, she froze. Her eyes rounded with shock as she felt something warm and wet soak the inside of her sweatpant legs.

"Oh!" One hand flew to her mouth, and grabbing Ben's shirtsleeve with the other, she made a stricken little sound. She stared into his eyes, which had widened with alarm.

"Ben," she said, "let's finish this conversation later. All right?"

Chapter Seven

"What is it?" While it was obvious something was wrong, Ben didn't immediately grasp the implications of Marcie's words and stunned expression.

"My water broke."

"Your wa—" Shocked into momentary incoherence, Ben gaped at her. He felt the blood drain from his face and couldn't formulate even one rational thought.

"But... but it's not time yet," he protested. "You yourself told me—"

"Ben, I know what I told you." Having gotten over the initial surprise, and faced now with the inevitable, Marcie was calm. "But having babies is not an exact science. Due dates tend to be iffy."

When he continued to just stand there, she gave his arm a little shake. "Ben! Get a grip. There's no need to panic because I haven't even had what you could call a con—owww...!"

Hit by her first real contraction just as she was trying to tell Ben that so far, she hadn't felt anything more
than a little twinge here and there, which she had as-
cribed to exertion and otherwise ignored, Marcie doubled over. She clutched her stomach and held her
breath as sweat popped out all over her body. Caught
completely off guard, she employed none of the tech-
niques she had taken such trouble to learn.

"Oh, oh," she moaned through gritted teeth, curling into herself and swaying back and forth while the
spasm seemed to go on and on. "Owie-owie-owie..."

"For God's sake, woman...!" Electrified by
Marcie's distress, Ben snapped into action. Once the
need was recognized, he was in his element, the charge-
taker. "Hang on."

He matter-of-factly pried one of her hands off her
stomach and firmly placed it around his waist. He held
it there with one hand while clamping his free arm
around her shoulders.

"Okay now, walk," he ordered, propelling her forward and ignoring her attempts to resist. "Breathe.
Don't hold it in. Puff it out.

"Atta girl," he praised when at last she responded
with a series of rapid breaths. "You're doing great."

"Ohh." Marcie's released a shaky sigh as the pain
receded. "You can stop shlepping me now." She dug
in her heels, though feebly since her knees still quaked
with reaction. "It's over."

"For the moment." Releasing her, Ben consulted his
watch. This, at least, was something he knew how to
do—managing, running things.

"Okay," he pronounced, "it's ten to four. I want
you to sit, rest and catch your breath. This early on it's

unlikely that the next contraction will be anytime soon.''

"Then right now would be too early, huh? Oowww...!''

Ben blinked, momentarily disconcerted by this unexpected turn of events. "But—"

"Yeah, I know," Marcie gasped, on her feet again and making a valiant effort to walk and breathe the way she should. "According to the book—*huff, huff, huff*—things shouldn't be happening this—damn, but this hurts!—fast. Tell that to Wiiidgeeet...!''

"Three minutes between contractions," Ben muttered with another quick check of his watch.

Wildly looking around, he raked a hand through his hair, his take-charge manner from moments ago reduced once again to panic. "Gotta call the doctor. But where the hell's the phone?"

"No phone," Marcie panted, walking and shallow-breathing with her face tilted up to the ceiling, "in this house. Anyway... no time. Can't wait for... doctor."

"What!" Though he resisted the idea with every fiber of his being, Ben knew she was right. The doctor, the hospital, were miles away. Meaning that he'd just been elected to play midwife.

Because the thought scared the living daylights out of him, he exploded. "Dammit, Marcie, I *knew* you shouldn't have been doing any cleaning!"

"Could you maybe yell at me later?" Marcie had sagged against the wall, for the moment without pain. "I really think we ought to hurry up and get me to someplace a bit cleaner...."

"To bed, right." Pulling himself together, Ben scooped her up in his arms and hurried out of the guesthouse. Trotting across the yard to the main house, he noticed that while he'd been talking to Marcie in the guesthouse, it had begun to snow. The stuff was coming down in a thick curtain of white and was already sticking to the ground.

"Just as well I don't have to drive you anywhere," he muttered. "We'd probably get stuck and I'd have to deliver the baby on the road."

"Always considerate...that's...me...." Marcie arms tightened around Ben's neck, signaling the onset of another contraction. She was all but strangling him as he crashed with her through the door into the kitchen.

"P-put me...down," Marcie said, panting, as breathless as if she were the one who had just jogged across the snowy yard.

Gently, Ben deposited her in the kitchen rocker.

Marcie said, "G-get a couple of...rubber—" With a keening wail, she gripped Ben's arm. "Oh, God, this hurts so. Oohhh, I want to..."

Her eyes widened, more in excitement than apprehension. "Ben! I don't believe this! I need to push!"

"Oh, God." He wasn't ready for this. What did he have to do? Hot water. "Marcie, don't do this. I gotta put water on to boil...."

"First get some rubber sheets. Hurry. I just changed the bed and I'll be damned...Oh, dear." She stopped to draw a series of shallow breaths, her face contorting with pain. "Never...mind...the sheets...."

Ben had already figured that out and was on his way with her to the bedroom. "Hold on, sweetheart," he murmured. "We can do this, you and I."

He yanked back the spread, carefully laid her on the bed and lingered for just a moment. Just long enough to smooth back her sweat-dampened curls and tell her how great he thought she was.

"Would you mind if I got Cookie to lend us a hand?" he asked. "He's delivered most of the foals and calves on this ranch."

Gritting her teeth, every sinew in her body straining as her insides twisted, Marcie mutely shook her head. Right at that moment, she wouldn't have cared if Ben called in the entire Montana State U. football squad, just as long as they knew about delivering babies.

Cookie was there in an instant. Leaving Ben to see to Marcie's immediate needs, he went about gathering all the supplies he figured he'd need, along with plenty of towels and hot water.

Ben secured one of Marcie's colorful scarves to the headboard and when the next contraction hit, told her to grab and hang on.

And after that, everything was pretty much a blur. Ben vaguely recalled being shoved aside as Cookie took over, and moments later Marcie's long-awaited Widget made her loudly protesting entrance into the world.

"A girl," Ben whispered to Marcie in an awed voice.

She gave him a tired but grateful grin. "I knew it would be."

"Just as well," Ben growled with mock ferocity. "Damn silly name—Widget—for a boy."

Marcie's weak chuckle turned into a grimace. "It hurts to laugh."

"It's damn great seeing you do it, though."

The look they exchanged was unguardedly warm and caring, the miracle they had shared having temporarily lowered all the barriers.

Both mother and baby had been cleaned up and made comfortable. Though exhausted from the rigors of giving birth, Marcie delayed a much-needed nap long enough to thank the two men who stood, beaming, but a little awkward now, too, at the foot of the bed.

The baby had been tucked into the old-fashioned cradle Marcie had found in the attic and restored shortly after her arrival at the Lazy H. Merely an arm's length away from her, the baby was peacefully asleep. A precious little cherub.

"I want to name her Jocelyn Haley Pauline," Marcie said. Her voice, though weak, was vibrant with affection and gratitude. "And I'd like the two of you to be her godfathers."

"Thanks, guys," she whispered, her eyelids drifting shut. "I owe ya."

She was asleep. Exchanging a glance—Cookie's eyes were suspiciously moist—the men quietly left the room.

"Come on into the study," Ben invited out in the hall. "I think we've earned us a drink."

"Well, sir, I reckon we did." Cookie blew loudly into his dark blue bandanna. "It's been a while since a child was borned on this spread."

"Have a seat," Ben said, pouring generous portions of bourbon into two glasses and handing one to the cook. "That would've been Chester, John Hillier's dad, wouldn't it?" He gestured with a bottle of Evian. "Water?"

Cookie declined mix of any kind, saying, "Chester, that's right, he come after yer mama. Couldn't wait t' leave the place, neither. Quite a blow to yer granddad, the way none o' the family felt tied t' the land."

They saluted each other and took a deep swallow.

"Yessir," Cookie said, nodding his head and smacking his lips in appreciation of the fine whisky, "your granddad woulda been mighty pleased t' know you came back here to stay."

He paused a beat and added, "An' I expect wi' the likes o' Miz Marcie by your side, there'll soon be a whole passel o' young'uns around to foller in yer footsteps. Does m' heart proud to be part of it, too."

"It does?" Ben asked, not in the least comfortable with the direction this conversation had taken.

"You bet." Cookie took another fortifying swallow. "That's a mighty fine thing you did, boss, marrying up with Miz Marcie'n all. Me'n the hands wish ye a lifetime o' happiness, an' we want ye to know that we respect ye and are mighty proud to be working the Lazy H by yer side."

It was the longest speech Ben had ever heard Cookie make and quite the accolade, given the old man's inherent reticence.

And it would have meant the world to Ben, *if* he had felt he deserved it. As it was, however, he couldn't bring himself to look Cookie Nichols in the eye. He looked down at his drink, no longer feeling very celebratory. He mumbled a gruff "Thanks."

The fact that Cookie seemed not to expect anything more than that—would, in fact, have been embarrassed by anything more emotional—did not make Ben feel any better about himself.

Because the fact was and would remain that there wasn't a snowball's chance in hell of Jocelyn Haley Pauline Kertin being raised here on the Lazy H. For the simple reason that both her mother and her appointed godfather had their own vision of the future, one that didn't include playing house with each other on a remote Montana ranch.

But could he say as much to Cookie? With a rueful sideways glance at his cook, Ben raised his glass to his mouth, drained it and thought, Hell, no.

They were snowed in for the first four days of little Josie's life. Ben had, of course, been on the phone to the doctor even as the drama of the baby's precipitous birth was unfolding—and getting some handy advice in the process. The arrangement they had agreed on was that Ben would drive Marcie and the baby into Missoula for a checkup, weigh-in and the like just as soon as the roads were passable.

In the meantime, since Marcie had planned to nurse the baby anyway, Doc Miller figured they'd make out just fine. Marcie hadn't been in any shape to voice an opinion and Ben had been too frazzled to worry about anything but the then and there.

Later, after Cookie had had a second drink and gone to his quarters, and while Ben had sat in his study without lights on, nursing his third, one of the things he had brooded about had been, Now what?

How was he to cope with a new mother and a help-less infant?

He hadn't been much of a hands-on father with Kirby. He had been too busy making money, both for his family and to get the ranch out of the red. And Jane had been the kind of woman who had very definite ideas about territories.

After they had gotten married, she had given up her teaching career because she wanted to devote herself completely to making a home for Ben. She had done a wonderful job of it, too, spoiling him completely. But also, in essence, erecting a sort of wall between them. A wall that signified, This is my stuff over here, yours is on the other side, and crossing over was by invitation only.

An invitation that was never issued.

During her pregnancy, Jane had made it clear that Kirby would be part of her territory. Small children needed their mothers, had been her position. Fathers didn't really figure very prominently until a kid was old enough to expand his or her field of exploration.

At the time, all of this had seemed reasonable to Ben. Jane had been a competent homemaker, a devoted mother. Her dedication had left him free to concentrate solely on the business.

He had enjoyed her pregnancy to the extent that she would allow him to share in it. He had been excited about the birth of his son and had adored the child, but had been content to let Jane be the primary caregiver. After all, he had continued to work eighteen-hour days, building and expanding the business.

So, what did he know about coping with a young mother and an infant? Nothing. Except that they scared him to death.

And yet he was responsible for them, for their well-being, at least until they had been checked by the doctor. True, the birth had been an easy one, as births went. Ben did remember Jane being in labor for many, many hours. She had suffered terribly, or so she had told him since she'd been adamant he not be allowed into the birthing room. She hadn't wanted him to see her in such immodest and undignified circumstances. Her words.

Now, looking back, and having just experienced firsthand the incredible miracle of birth, Ben wished he had not let himself be dissuaded from participating more in Kirby's birth. And in the early years of his life.

He had such few memories of good times shared with his young son. It was one of the reasons the loss of him had been such a blow. He had looked forward so to the time when Jane would deem Kirby old enough to spend one-on-one time with his father.

But the time had never come and the opportunity to do better the next time, to try and make up for his mistakes with his first child by lavishing as much time, love and attention on the second, had not been granted him, either.

Jane had been adamant about not ever wanting to go through something as traumatic as childbirth again. They had fought about it, often and bitterly. Because, having been an only child himself and so lonely and alone after his parents' death, Ben had wanted Kirby to have the comfort and companionship of siblings in the event something should ever happen to Jane and him.

But Jane would have none of it. She had insisted Ben have a vasectomy because, she said, it was the only foolproof protection around. When he refused, she had forbidden him her bed. And later, even though he had submitted to the surgery that would leave him sterile, she had left him....

With a groan, Ben covered his eyes. And for once he didn't try to keep back the tears he had never before allowed himself to shed.

He was alone in his dark study, he was emotionally and physically exhausted and he was heartsick with remorse and wishful thinking. If only he could turn back the clock....

But he couldn't. And so maybe it *was* time to weep, time to make peace with himself. Time to forgive himself and to go on.

Because maybe, just maybe, he had been given another chance.

Slowly Ben lowered his hand. It dropped to dangle between his knees as he stared sightlessly into the dark. A face, pale and freckled and framed by a riot of Titian curls rose in front of his mental eye.

Marcie.

His *wife.* To have and to hold. Forever?

It was a scary thought, but . . .

It wasn't long before Marcie was awakened by a screaming baby.

Ben, in the kitchen with Cookie who had announced that he would take complete charge of Miz Marcie and the boss's well-being, was at her side in a flash.

And a good thing, too, since he caught Marcie in the process of getting out of bed.

"Whoa there, young lady," he scolded. "And just where do you think you're going?"

"To the bathroom and then—"

"Not on your own you're not." Matter-of-factly, Ben scooped her robe off the foot of the bed and draped it around Marcie's shoulders. "I'll carry you."

"You will not!" Though an attack of modesty at this stage of the game might be like shutting the barn door after the cow has run out, Marcie figured Enough already. "I'm perfectly capable—Benedict Kertin, you put me down this instant!"

Ben did, as carefully as if she were as fragile as a precious porcelain doll, at the bathroom door.

"Call me when you're ready to come out," he told her sternly. "I know you think you're a superwoman, but I won't have you coming to harm under my roof before you've seen the doctor."

"But afterward it's okay?" Marcie quipped sourly, and shut the door in Ben's face. By the time she had done the necessary and freshened up, however, her legs shook like jelly and her head felt light. She had to hold on to the counter and then the towel holder as she made her way to the door.

"Ben?"

Ben had gone to pick up and comfort the baby but, at Marcie's call, thrust little Josie at Cookie.

"Just hold her," he instructed, already on his way. "I'll be right back."

At the bathroom, he scooped Marcie up in his arms. For once, she didn't protest.

"I hate to say this because you'll probably be impossible to live with," Marcie said, gratefully letting her head come to rest against his shoulder, "but you were right about my not being ready to, you know..."

"Climb Mount Everest?" Ben supplied with a grin. "Don't worry about it. You've got all kinds of help here."

Marcie saw what he meant when they got back to the bedroom. With his arms stiffly extended in front of him and a petrified expression on his face, Cookie was holding the still squalling infant as though it were a hand grenade about to go off.

"Jeez, boss," he sputtered as soon as Ben walked into the room, "you oughtn't to have jest handed me this child like that. I ain't never held no young'un afore."

"Can't say I've had a helluva lot of practice myself, old-timer." Ben got Marcie settled and then gently took the baby out of the cook's shaking hands. "But I figure between the three of us we oughta be able to swing it."

Muttering to himself, Cookie beat a hasty retreat.

Ben placed little Josie in Marcie's eager arms. "By the sound of things, I think your daughter is in need of something neither Cookie nor I can give her," he said, his voice roughened by the powerful emotions the picture of Marcie with her child evoked. A Madonna with a red halo of curls. And the little one, quiet now, already rooting against her mother's breast in search of sustenance.

"I'll go upstairs and bring down diapers and stuff," he said awkwardly. "We'll need to change her after she's done."

"We?" Marcie asked, between tender cooings to her child.

"Yes, well..." Ben cleared his throat and averted his eyes. "I, uh... That is, if you don't mind, I'd, uh, like to help with..."

With a shrug, feeling way out of his element and more than a little vulnerable, he stalked to the door.

"Ben."

Already on the threshold, Ben turned when Marcie called his name. Her expression was full of tenderness and her smile trembled around the edges.

"I'd love your help," she said softly. "I'm new at this mother thing and it scares me to death. But maybe between the two of us we won't blow it completely. What do you say?"

Unable to speak, Ben compressed his lips and gave a curt nod. But he looked at Marcie as if she had just handed him all the riches in the world.

The Monday after Thanksgiving, a little over a week after Josie's birth, they made the trip to the doctor. By then Marcie was heartily sick of inactivity, lounging around and being fussed over, which was the regimen Ben made sure she maintained. He was almost paranoid in his worry over her and the baby's well-being.

The holiday had been a joyous affair though Marcie, Ben and Cookie Nichols had broken tradition by not eating with the rest of the Lazy H staff and workers this year. They had shared a quiet, but festive turkey dinner in the cozy ranch-house kitchen.

There was still plenty of snow around but, by all reports, the roads were in good condition and the weather was supposed to stay cold and dry for the next twenty-four hours at least.

They made the near seventy-mile drive to Missoula in good time, a little less than two hours. Road conditions were not conducive to pushing the pedal to the metal.

Ben had secured the baby carrier to the Bronco's front seat and had wanted Marcie to lie down on the seat behind them.

But Marcie had put her foot down. Apart from some unpredictable mood swings, some bouts of inexplicable melancholy, she felt perfectly healthy and fit. She declared that she would dress for the occasion and that she would ride sitting up. Like a person, she had told Ben, brandishing the diaper bag like a warrior's shield in front of her.

Since her figure had in no way regained its prepregnancy dimensions, she had put on the outfit Ben had bought for her on the occasion of Rosalie James's visit. They had not as yet seen hide or hair of the photographs that had been taken.

Having critically studied herself in the mirror, Marcie decided that the dress looked even better on her now than before. And the flash of something more than mere admiration in Ben's eyes had thrillingly confirmed that assessment.

After months of shapeless castoffs, followed more recently by days spent largely in a nightgown and robe, Marcie was more than ready for a little glamour. She had fussed with her hair, which had grown to shoulder length, scooping the mass of curls up off her neck and securing it at the back of her head with a cloisonné barrette that had been a gift from an artisan she'd known in L.A. And she had also applied some light makeup.

She considered her efforts had been worth it when she heard Ben's sharp intake of breath at the sight of her.

"After we're done at the doctor's," Ben was saying as they drove up Missoula's busy Broadway toward the medical center where Dr. Miller had his office, "and if he gives you and Josie a clean bill of health, let's go to the mall and grab some lunch. Would you like that?"

"Do birds fly?" Marcie quipped. She dearly loved to rattle Ben's cage. For all he had loosened up around her considerably, as far as Marcie was concerned, there were far too many times when he grew serious and self-contained. "I feel like I've just been sprung out of prison."

She knew Ben had misunderstood her meaning completely when she caught his suddenly shuttered gaze in the rearview mirror.

"Ranch life starting to pale?" he drawled in the deliberately deprecating tone of voice that never failed to light Marcie's fuse.

"Dammit, Kertin—"

She bit back the rest of her exclamation when the baby started to wail. Once again her gaze collided with Ben's in the rearview mirror. This time his eyes clearly said, *See what you've done?* before he swung them toward little Jocelyn with a soothing murmur.

Which ticked Marcie right off. "It's not ranch life I'm having a problem with," she told Ben stiffly. "It's being allowed *no* life at all that's giving me a pain."

"Tired of motherhood already?"

"No. And quit putting words in my mouth." Honestly, Marcie fumed, there were times when she would dearly love to pick up a skillet and brain him. "But ever since Widget's arrival you haven't let me indulge in anything *but* motherhood."

"I've helped out wherever I could."

"Well, of course you have. That's not the point."

"Then what is?"

Marcie slumped in her seat and muttered a defeated "Darned if I know."

Postpartum blues, Dr. Miller told her when she mentioned the letdown feeling, the bouts of melancholy and irritability, as well as the guilt that accompanied those times when she felt a definite lack of joy in motherhood.

"It's perfectly normal," he assured her. "Part of the hormonal changes taking place in your body, don't you know. It'll sort itself out in no time. You'll see."

Well, that was a relief, Marcie thought, as was the doctor's assurance that she and little Jocelyn were in great shape.

"You did a fine job, Mr. Kertin." The doctor jocularly clapped Ben on the shoulder after he accompanied Marcie out to where Ben had been waiting in the outer office. "I'll be sure to keep you in mind," he added humorously, "the next time I need an assistant in obstetrics."

"No, thanks." Ben chuckled. "I don't think my nerves would be up to a repeat performance."

While Marcie bundled the baby back into layers of outdoor clothes and warm blankets, Ben lowered his voice to ask the doctor, "Does my, uh, wife seem happy to you?"

After giving Ben a startled look that immediately changed to one of shrewd comprehension, Doc Miller said, "Just a minute," and strode away.

He returned moments later and pressed a small booklet into Ben's hand. "Read this," he advised. "You'll find everything you need to know about new mothers explained in there."

Outside, a sharp northerly wind made the temperature seem well below the posted twenty-eight degrees Fahrenheit. With only the light blazer of her outfit to shield her from it, Marcie couldn't keep her teeth from chattering as she, Ben and Josie got out of the Bronco and hurried across the parking lot toward Southgate Mall.

"First order of business is getting you a coat," Ben decreed in a voice that brooked no argument.

"Consider it an early Christmas present," he added when Marcie nevertheless opened her mouth to object.

Christmas. Marcie's mouth closed with a snap. Darn it, it was right around the corner! With everything that had happened, she had given no thought to the holidays ahead.

It struck her then that this would be her first holiday in years without John, and everything came rush-

ing back. The way they had parted, exchanging words
of anger and accusation instead of goodbyes.

Remembering, wishing things could have been different, her eyes filled.

When she didn't speak, Ben, lugging the baby carrier, tossed her a sideways glance. He was shocked to
see her tears. Aware that it didn't take much these days
to make Marcie cry and thinking it was the coat thing
that had made her upset, he said with some exasperation, "For heaven's sake, Marcie, be reasonable."

He stopped dead, stunned, when in response, Marcie
turned on her heel with a sob and ran back to the car.

What had he said?

Completely at a loss, Ben stood irresolute. He
glanced down at the baby he was holding, then back at
Marcie who had reached the Bronco and stood next to
it with her head bowed.

Surely this couldn't be about the coat.

So what else had he said? Ben wracked his brain.
Christmas? Yeah, but...?

Frowning, wondering if every man felt this helpless
around an overwrought woman, and wishing he were
faced with something as simple as a hostile corporate
takeover instead of this emotional crisis, Ben strode
back to the Bronco.

"Marcie?" Her back was to him. Ben shifted the
baby carrier to free one of his hands. Tentatively he
touched her shoulder. "Was it something I said?"

Her answer was a half shrug, or maybe it was just a
listless effort to dislodge his hand, accompanied by
something strangled and unintelligible.

"Do you want to go home?"

"Home?" The sound she made was a ragged half
sob, half laugh. And the look she tossed him held so

much despair, Ben felt like he'd been punched in the solar plexus.

"Tell me, Ben," she said, her voice little more than an aching rasp, "where exactly is that?"

"What do you mean?" What had brought this on? Ben wondered with more than a little despair of his own. Ever since little Josie had been born, it seemed, that daily, Marcie had grown more...despondent. Fleetingly, he wondered what kind of light Doc Miller's pamphlet might shed on the subject. But however much it was, it didn't help him here and now. "Your home is at the Lazy H, of course."

"Of course." Her little laugh was bitter. "But for how much longer, now that you've gotten your hands on my child?"

Chapter Eight

If Marcie had turned around and slugged him, Ben couldn't have been more thunderstruck. And, yes, dammit, hurt. Even angry.

He uttered something short and vile beneath his breath. And then, through clenched teeth, he ground out, "Look, lady, whatever this is about, I'm not going to stand here and freeze my toes off while you're having your little crisis."

He stalked to the other side of the car. Awkwardly balancing the baby carrier, he unlocked the door with a not-quite-steady hand. His motions jerky with suppressed fury at the unfairness of Marcie's accusations, he went about fastening the carrier onto the seat. All the while he sliced quick, angry glances in Marcie's direction.

Still hovering next to the Bronco on the other side, Marcie seethed with hurts and resentments of her own.

Little crisis, she thought, angrily swiping at unwelcome tears. Yeah. Sure.

Here she was feeling as if the bottom had dropped out of her world and *he* had the gall to refer to it as a little crisis.

Okay. So maybe she had been just a *tad* unfair to him. So maybe she didn't *really* believe Ben meant to rob her of her child. But she was so afraid. Afraid because she was so darn vulnerable. Couldn't he see that? Her future was uncertain, she had just given birth, her child's father was dead and she was living on another man's charity. Surely that was enough to drive *any* woman to despair?

Still . . . Marcie sniffled, fumbling for a tissue. Ben had been good. He had tried. And he didn't deserve her sniping at him. Nor did he deserve her insulting innuendo of moments before.

Dabbing at her nose, wishing she would learn to curb her tongue, Marcie furtively watched Ben stride back to her side of the truck. She took in the rigid set of his shoulders, the tight set of his mouth and the shuttered expression and knew it masked his justifiable hurt and affront.

"Ben." Her voice squeaked, and she swallowed, taking a tentative step toward him when he stopped at the Bronco's rear door. "I . . . I'm truly sorry."

"Yeah." Ben's expression didn't ease. The quick glance he shot her as he opened the door was grim. "So am I."

Face turned, he gestured for Marcie to get in the truck.

Marcie took another step closer, but otherwise didn't comply. She put a hand on his arm and didn't remove it when he pointedly glanced down at it. "Forgive me, Ben."

Her voice breaking, she added, "Please?"

"Dammit, Marcie—" Ben's head snapped up, eyes blazing, lips parted for a scathing retort. But he abruptly closed his mouth when he saw the desolation in Marcie's gaze.

With a harshly muttered curse, he turned away, inhaling and expelling several audible breaths as he visibly struggled for composure.

Miserable, Marcie watched and waited. Her teeth dug into her lower lip; her heart was in her shoes.

Only to shoot up into her throat seconds later when Ben, with a strangled "Oh, hell!" hauled her into a bone-crushing hug.

Reflexively, Marcie's arms went around him and she hung on as though for dear life. "I'm a shrew," she whispered.

"Yeah. One that's shaking with cold." Ben tightened his hold and pressed his cheek against the crown of her curls for just a moment. God, but this woman could turn him inside out. "Come on," he said gruffly. "What say we go buy you that damned winter coat."

A couple of hours later they were lingering over coffee. A stylish, but practical coat had been purchased, and they, as well as little Josie, had had their lunch. With the baby now contentedly asleep between them on the seat of their secluded corner booth, Marcie and Ben were talking.

That is, Marcie was talking. Ben merely listened, though "merely" was a gross understatement of the intensity with which he attended every one of Marcie's words.

She was telling him about her childhood, after he had deftly maneuvered the conversation in that direction when the topic of Josie's care and feeding—always a popular one for them—had been duly exhausted.

"I guess I was always a handful," Marcie was ruefully confiding. "Crises of any kind had a way of bringing out the worst in me.

"They still do," she added, slanting Ben a glance. "As you've noticed."

Their gazes held a moment. Ben didn't speak, but his expression encouraged Marcie to go on. She looked down at her hands, cradling the mug of cooling coffee.

"When my parents...died, I threw what, in retrospect, can only be described as a two-year temper tantrum," she said. "I was furious with them.

"How's that for idiotic?" She raised her eyes with a hollow, self-deprecating little laugh.

Ben didn't answer, only reached across the table to give her arm a reassuring squeeze as he quietly asked, "What did you do?"

"You mean outside of terrorizing my foster parents, the other kids, skipping school, shoplifting and generally making a royal pain of myself?"

Pushing away the coffee she no longer wanted, Marcie straightened up in her seat. Her expression turned wry. "I met Bobo Vegada. And I discovered art. Sculpting."

She waved a hand in dismissal. "But that was later. First, I raised hell whenever and wherever I could. I wanted to punish my parents."

"I know," Ben said.

Marcie nodded. She was sure that he *did* know. She curled her hands into fists, feeling again the familiar pain and frustration. "I didn't, of course. Any more than I am now able to punish John for leaving me— alone, pregnant. And broke."

Closing her eyes, Marcie drew a shuddering breath, the scene with John as vivid as life in her mind.

"His final words to me were an ultimatum," she said. "'It or me,' he told me. 'The choice is yours.' And then he left."

Ben sat motionless, grimly staring out of the restaurant window into an ever-thickening curtain of falling snow.

"There was no...goodbye," Marcie went on. "No phone call. He was furious with me."

"For getting pregnant?" If John had been around, Ben would have cheerfully beaten him to a pulp. "Seems to me he had something to do with that, too."

Marcie shook her head. "He'd always been adamant about never wanting children. And I had promised—"

"*You* promised?" Ben flared. "*He* couldn't take care of some birth control?"

"Don't," Marcie said. "John was John. *He* didn't change."

"But you did," Ben concluded, grimly thinking that John had always been John, all right. Long on charm and a thirst for adventure, but quick to take a powder when it came time to pay the piper. As boys, whenever John came to stay at the ranch, it had always been Ben who had suffered the consequences of his cousin's many pranks and practical jokes.

"Yeah," Marcie said softly, sadly, still looking down at her hands. "I changed. Or, more correctly, my priorities did. Maybe it had to do with that biological clock women my age become obsessed with.''

She gave a humorless little laugh and shook her head. ''I don't know. Last year, for some reason, I started noticing babies, and children. And I got envious. I developed a longing for stability, for roots.''

She raised her head to discover that Ben's eyes glittered with a myriad of emotions that were too complex to sort out or decipher, but which struck a chord just the same.

''Our fast-paced, freewheeling kind of marriage suddenly wasn't right for me anymore, but John blew his stack every time I as much as hinted at settling down,'' she said quietly. ''So I got cute and decided to present him with a fait accompli.''

She looked down at her hands again. ''Ben, the man was thirty-eight years old. The *Los Angeles Times* had offered him a great job for the umpteenth time. If he took it, there would have been no need for him to travel any longer. I thought a child . . .''

She shook her head, still amazed even now at her own stupidity. ''I was a fool,'' she said, so softly, Ben had to strain to hear it. ''And so I lost. Everything.''

''You have a beautiful baby daughter,'' Ben reminded her with quiet forcefulness, thinking that he would give anything to have his own child, to have Kirby, alive.

''Yes.'' Marcie didn't look at Josie, still peacefully asleep. She continued to somberly contemplate her hands. ''Yes, I do have a beautiful baby daughter.''

But nothing else, she was thinking.

''You also have your health and people who care about you,'' Ben said as if in answer to her silent lament.

With a sharp frown at Marcie's slumped shoulders and bowed head, he decided to be brutal for her own good. "So pull yourself together," he said sternly. "Quit feeling sorry for yourself."

As he had hoped, his harshness brought Marcie's head up with a snap. "Is that what you think I'm doing?" she charged, shocked and hurt. "Feeling sorry for myself?"

"Frankly, yes." Since he was feeling pretty sorry for her, too, it took some effort for Ben to sound as cold and unfeeling as he did. Only the realization that a continued show of sympathy and commiseration on his part would hinder rather than help Marcie come to grips with her guilt and grief made it possible.

And so he steeled himself against the look of betrayal he glimpsed in her eyes. Grimly, he said, "I've got news for you, Marcie. Life goes on, and I suggest you get on with yours. Stop looking back."

"As you are doing?"

Though Marcie had spoken barely above a whisper, her words hit Ben like a bullet between the eyes. Already in the act of sliding out of the booth, he went stock-still.

"We were discussing you," he said with cold finality. "Not me."

"I know." It cost Marcie to raise her chin and meet Ben's smoldering gaze with a determined one of her own. "And it's always easier to dish out advice than to swallow it, isn't it?"

With Marcie's pithy observation to chew on, Ben stepped on the gas pedal with more force than was prudent, given the fact that several inches of snow had accumulated during the time they had spent in the mall.

The Bronco fishtailed wildly in spite of its four-wheel drive.

"Dammit, Kertin, get a grip," he muttered, bringing the truck back under control. If there'd been more traffic, they could have been in trouble. As it was, the road was a lot slicker than he had thought. With some sixty miles still to go till they reached the Lazy H, and the snow coming down at a fast and furious clip, he now wondered if they'd make it.

Behind him, in the back seat, Marcie sat huddled into her new coat. A quick glance in the rearview mirror showed Ben that she was white-faced and apprehensive.

"Relax," he said. "This isn't the first storm we've weathered together, now is it? And it sure's heck won't be the last."

He held Marcie's gaze just long enough to make her realize the double meaning had been intended. And then he added, "If we take it slow, I'm sure we'll make it."

"Will we?" Marcie asked even as Ben's gaze flicked back to the road before once again briefly connecting with hers.

"Don't you want to?" he countered.

"I'm scared," Marcie said.

"Of what? Making it? Or failing?"

"Neither." Marcie huddled more deeply into her coat, cold even though the heater was doing a more than adequate job of warming the Bronco's interior. "Or maybe," she added, suppressing a shiver, "maybe I should say both."

"Well, if it's any consolation to you—" Once more their eyes met as Ben said, "So am I, lady. So am I."

Not much later Ben decided, Enough was enough. It was snowing so hard, he could barely see two feet ahead, and the faltering light of approaching dusk didn't help matters, either.

"We're going to have to get off the road," he announced, peering intently ahead. He figured they were about three miles or so from Kingsley. Which wasn't a town exactly, more like a random collection of houses around a ramshackle service station. But it did have a motel. Since conditions were worsening with every passing mile, he planned for them to stay in Kingsley and wait things out. At least until daylight, when visibility would be somewhat improved.

"Help me watch for the Kingsley turnoff," he said to Marcie who had scooted forward and was leaning across the backrest of the passenger seat, petting an increasingly restless Josie.

"There," she exclaimed, pointing, just as Ben saw it, too.

ValeVu Motel.

The garish neon sign was reduced to shades of palest pastel by the filter of thickly falling snow, but visible. And heartily welcome.

"Think they'll have room?" Marcie asked anxiously. Much as she trusted in Ben's driving skills and the Bronco's four-wheel drive, she didn't relish the prospect of continuing on to the ranch and possibly renewing her acquaintance with a roadside ditch. "Think there'll be a vacancy?"

"We'll soon find out." Ben drove to a stop in front of the sign that flashed Office. "Be right back."

He opened the door and slid from behind the wheel. The icy blast of snowy air that hit the interior lingered to bathe Marcie in damply frosty shivers. With her precious little Widget quiet for the moment, she subsided back in her own seat, tugging the collar of her coat high up around her chin.

Her precious little Widget.

Marcie bit down hard on her lower lip as she wondered, bleakly, how often in the past few days she had thought of her daughter in those loving terms. Less and less, it seemed now on sober reflection.

Instead of rejoicing in the child she had so fervently wanted, and paid so dearly for in terms of personal losses, she had spent her time agonizing about herself and about a past that could not be changed.

A past she *wouldn't* change, given the chance.

For she knew now, could admit now, that John, had he stuck around instead of flying off in a selfish rage, would have been no help with this child. On the contrary, he would have resented poor little Widget for interfering with his life-style.

The fact that he had gotten himself killed in the aftermath of his—*all right, Marcie, let's call it what it really was*—his temper tantrum, didn't change the fact that had he stayed, he would have been a rotten father.

He had known that about himself. Just as he had known that their brief marriage was not only in the doldrums, it had floundered on the rocks of their dichotomous priorities.

And *she* had known it, too.

But she had gone ahead and gotten herself pregnant anyway, which meant she had made a conscious choice away from John and toward this child.

So did that mean his death was on her conscience?

No. Only a complete masochist would continue to think so. Because John, too, had made a conscious choice. He had wanted to be away from her and away from the responsibility of fatherhood. And he had been brutally, insultingly, honest about it.

How had he put it?

"Even if this kid you're carrying really *is* mine— something I've got serious doubts about, by the way— get rid of it. And maybe then we'll talk, but not before."

And when Marcie had balked—in truth, she had hit the roof—John had offered his ultimatum and stalked out.

So was it her fault John had died?

A chilly draft enveloped her and ruffled her curls as once again a door was opened. She raised her head and stared bleakly at Ben. A frown formed on his brow as he caught that stare.

"Quit beating up on yourself," he growled, deftly unstrapping the baby carrier, and amazing Marcie with the clarity of his perception. "We all live, or die, with our choices. John was no exception."

He hoisted the carrier and picked up the tote full of Josie's supplies. "I'll be back for you in a minute," he told Marcie. "Don't move."

True to his word, Ben was back in a flash, bundling Marcie into his arms and carrying her toward the motel unit next to the manager's office.

Marcie didn't even attempt to object. Aside from the fact that she knew from previous experience that to protest was futile, her dressy shoes were no match for the foot or more of snow through which she would have had to slosh.

Lips compressed, eyes squinting against the driving snow, Ben covered the short distance from Bronco to musty-smelling motel room at a near trot, jouncing Marcie like a sack of meal as he went.

Marcie clung to the sturdy column of his neck and ducked her face to avoid the needle-sharp pricks inflicted by the snow.

Josie, awake now and kicking up a storm of her own in the carrier seat that sat in the middle of the room's only bed, greeted her mother's arrival with an ear-splitting wail.

"Hungry, I'll bet," Ben said, setting Marcie on her feet without ceremony. "I'll leave you to it," he added and left Marcie to gape after him as he strode from the room without another word, shutting the door behind himself with a very final-sounding *thud*.

So. Swallowing hard as she continued to stare in shock at the closed door, Marcie sank down at the edge of the mattress. One of her hands groped in back of her for Josie's carrier and automatically patted the baby in a comforting fashion.

But her mind was not on the task. It was on the man who, she was suddenly convinced, had just walked out of her life for good.

Chapter Nine

Ben was in the motel office, calling the ranch. There were no phones in the individual rooms. He had just received a very upsetting piece of news from Roger Stevens: Chester Hillier had arrived at the ranch via helicopter just ahead of the snowstorm.

Ben was still chewing on this, wondering what it meant and how Marcie was going to react when his manager said, "And before I forget, Ben—Judge Claymore left a message to give him a call. ASAP. Here's his number...."

Ben jotted it down, murmuring, "Fine. Thanks. Bye." He hung up the phone, but didn't move. With his forehead deeply furrowed, he stared down at the slip of paper and thought, Hell. First Chester and now Judge Claymore, the man who had married Marcie and him. One was bound to mean trouble, but what in blazes could the judge want with them?

"How're you coming with that coffee?" he asked Nora Franklin, the woman who ran the ValeVu Motel. He stuck the scrap of paper with Claymore's number into his pocket with the idea of dealing with it later. As to Chester—well, he'd have to be dealt with later, too. Like tomorrow, when they got back to the ranch. Right now his first priority was to get Marcie and the baby squared away.

After which he supposed he and Marcie had better take time for a strategy session.

"All done, and here ye go." Nora, weathered and lean from years in the prairie sun, shoved a battered thermos past her husband, Elroy, then reached back for some plastic mugs. "Come back for your supper in about an hour, give or take. But don't let it git around, mind. I don't want ever'one of our guests linin' up here for grub."

"I won't," Ben promised, accepting the mugs and the thermos. "And thank you kindly."

"Tell the wife to holler if she needs somethin' for the baby," the old woman called after him as he went out the door.

Ben touched a finger to the brim of his hat, then quickly ducked next door to unit number one where he'd left Marcie. He went to turn the handle, but it wouldn't move. Marcie had locked the door. And the key, Ben recalled, lay on that brown, arborite-covered monstrosity that passed for a table.

Buffeted by the wind and pelted with hurtful pellets of snow, he flat-handed the door. He called Marcie's name, but the wind tore the word from his lips and swallowed the sound.

It seemed to take forever, and quite a bit of pounding, before his summons was answered and the door opened a crack. One large, red-rimmed brown eye peered out at him before, with a choked little cry, Marcie opened the door just wide enough to let Ben squeeze through.

"You're back," she said weakly, clutching the front of her dress, which was unbuttoned. It seemed his knocks had interrupted the feeding of her daughter who now lay howling in the middle of the bed, arms and legs thrashing.

Marcie took a couple of steps back on not-quite-steady legs. Her relief at seeing Ben was almost as painful as her earlier sense of loss had been.

"I thought you had—" Turning away, she caught herself with a quick shake of the head and a choked little laugh.

"Good grief, Widget," she exclaimed, and hurried to pick up the squalling infant. She cuddled her close and made soothing noises, feeling almost giddy from a sudden surge of happiness. "She does go on, doesn't she?"

Ben closed the door and set down the thermos and mugs. He shrugged out of his coat, which had already begun to drip as the snow melted in the warmth of the room.

"You thought I'd what?" he asked, carefully carrying the jacket into the adjoining bathroom and draping it over the chipped and water-stained claw-footed tub.

"Oh, nothing." No way was Marcie going to admit to thinking she had been abandoned when, obviously, he had only gone to get them some coffee.

With Josie draped over one shoulder, she awkwardly finished buttoning her dress. "Is the weather improving at all?"

"No." Ben was at the bathroom sink, washing his hands. Walking Josie, Marcie furtively watched him. He had put his dripping hat next to his coat on the tub and now, after drying his hands, he ran them through his hat-flattened shock of midnight-black hair.

She was struck, not for the first time, by how ruggedly attractive he was. And how totally—endearingly, to her—unaware he seemed to be of that fact.

His expression preoccupied, Ben gave himself no more than a cursory once-over in the mirror, and caught her watching him.

Holding her gaze in the mirror, he said flatly, "You thought I had left you."

"No, I . . ." Needing to look away, Marcie turned to lay Josie on the bed. She rummaged in the carryall and brought out a diaper. "It's just that . . ."

"You thought I had left you," Ben repeated more forcefully as he angrily tossed the hand towel into the sink. Walking back into the room, he regarded her coldly, saying, "In spite of everything that's passed, you still think I'm such a louse, I'd go back on my word."

"Ben, no." Marcie straightened; she turned entreatingly toward him. "It's not like that. It's because of *me*. It's because I've been such a pill all day and—"

"We're *married*, Marcie," Ben scathingly interrupted. "That means something to me, even if the deal was for one year only."

"Ben, I *know* that. And—"

"But if you have a problem with that," Ben went on, cutting her off, "then now is the time to speak up. As a matter of fact—"

Ben abruptly stopped talking as, suddenly, it seemed of the utmost importance to do something about Judge Claymore's message. If there was more bad news to be had—and his gut told him there was—then perhaps now was the best time to deal with that, too.

He strode past Marcie to the bathroom and snatched up his hat and coat. "There's something I have to do."

"What is it?" Marcie was watching him with growing alarm. "Where're you going?"

"To make a call."

"But—" She didn't want him to go. She was wound as tight as a spring, filled with a strange and unsettling sense of foreboding. They needed to talk. She needed . . . "Ben, please. . . ."

But Ben stopped only long enough to pick the key up off the table. "I won't be long," he said. "And I'll bring you back something to eat. . . ."

By the time Ben came back close to an hour later carrying a covered tray, Marcie had settled Josie in the makeshift bed she had fashioned by pushing the room's one armchair flush against the wall.

"Ben." She started toward him the moment he stepped in the door. But a foot or so away from him, she stopped, suddenly uncertain.

He looked so withdrawn, and more forbidding than he had in a long time.

"Oh, Ben, what's wrong?"

"In a minute." Ben set the tray on the table. "Here's some supper for you."

"Ben." He turned to her with a questioning frown and she said, "I don't want any supper. I want..."

You. The word hung between them, unspoken, but palpable and raw. Ben stood transfixed, momentarily unable to move or respond. Marcie's face, he noted with a pang, looked pale and drawn. Distress and something else had darkened her eyes until they were almost as black as his own.

Need. That's what was there in her eyes. A need as powerful as his own. A need he would give everything to be able to give in to, respond to.

But he didn't. Couldn't. Not before they had talked. Not before they had established some boundaries of trust or before he had told her about the conversation he'd just had with Judge Claymore.

And not before she then said the words, the only words, that could render Judge Claymore's shocking disclosure immaterial.

He shook his head, as much to clear it as in denial to Marcie's—and his own—needs and wants. Lamely, he gestured toward the dinner tray. "It's...chili, you know. Maybe if you—dammit, Marcie!"

Aware of her, drawn to her, he swung around and faced her. Faced her eyes, bright with unshed tears and full of longing.

He would have had to be dead not to respond to the longing. He had never felt more alive.

"Marcie." Her name an agonized murmur, Ben went to her, wrapped his arms around her and drew her into his heat.

Marcie tipped back her head, seeking his gaze. Their eyes locked, looked deep, searched. Their pulses sped up. They felt each other's heartbeat as though it were their own. They breathed each other's breath. Poised on the brink of something new, something grand, they hesitated.

And then Marcie, with a shaky sigh, closed her eyes and boldly captured Ben's mouth with her own.

For a moment, an eternity, nothing happened. Ben did not react. He stood tall and straight and statue-still, his arms clamped around her, his mouth closed against the gentle exploration of Marcie's tongue.

And then, with a groan, his lips parted, possessed, plundered. His tongue welcomed hers. One hand shifted to slide across her back, there to stroke and caress and urge her more fully against his strength.

Marcie's hands, too, were busy. They contoured his shoulders, feverishly traced the hardness of sinew and muscle beneath the soft flannel shirt. As the kiss deepened, as their tongues explored and their bodies pressed closer, her splayed fingers slid up his neck and tunneled into his hair, gripping handfuls of it and holding him still for her passionate kiss.

Kissing Ben, being kissed by him in return, was everything she could have dreamed. It was fire, glorious and hot. It was wild, it was delicious, it was abandoned. Yet at the same time it was sweet and tender in ways Marcie would never have dreamed it could be.

It was powerful in that it satisfied one craving while at the same time giving birth to ever-stronger wants and needs so that, when at last they parted for breath, the wants and needs were still there. And stronger than before.

"Oh, Ben," Marcie breathed, and something shifted inside Ben at her dreamy smile and slightly unfocused gaze. "I hoped it would be like this."

"Not me," Ben murmured, his gaze sliding to her sweetly curved lips, still glistening and puffy from his kiss. "I *knew* it would be like this."

Reason told him they had to talk. That he should tell her about the phone call and what it meant, could mean, for both of them.

But somehow, with the feel of her soft and pliant in his arms, reason was the last thing he wanted to listen to.

"What are you doing to me, Marcie-girl?" he asked in a husky whisper, holding her close, her head tucked beneath his chin, and feeling her heartbeat match his own.

"Doing?" Marcie drew back a little so she could look at him. What was he thinking? she wondered. What was he feeling? Had their kiss meant anything to him beyond the physical? Had it made clear to him, as it had to her, the fact that the easiest thing in the world would be to fall in love?

That, in fact, in her case she very much feared it was already too late. She *had* fallen. For him. She *did* love. Him.

Was any of this going through his mind? Was it in his heart? His expression gave nothing away.

Troubled, immeasurably saddened by his apparent need to keep shutting her out, Marcie wanted nothing so much as to shake him up by confronting him with her love. To demand he declare himself and that they go on from there.

But, looking up into his shuttered face, some instinct warned her the time was not right. That she should keep it light, for both their sakes.

She didn't stop to analyze why that should be, only reminded herself that her intuition had rarely failed her.

"It's been such a crazy day," she said. "I'm all shook up, and I was so scared. I needed ... something. Some reassurance, some comfort. And there you were."

She shrugged, giving him a purposely abashed, sheepish little grin. "I guess one thing just led to another."

"Just like that."

"Uh-huh." Marcie found it difficult to keep up the insouciant facade with Ben staring at her so relentlessly. "Haven't you ever done anything impulsive?" she asked.

"By impulsive, do you mean without a good reason?"

"Nooo." She would have liked to move, to get away from his too-unsettling proximity, but Ben still had his arms around her, loosely, and somehow Marcie didn't think he would let her slip away. "I mean impulsive, as in not analyzing a thing to death before doing it."

"And have you always been impulsive?"

"Pretty much, yes."

"Without fear of consequences?"

"Weeell ..." Staring back at him, she caught the glint of humor in his eyes and narrowed her own. "Is that a trick question?"

"Maybe." Ben tightened his arms around her and drew her against him. Flush against him.

"There are always consequences," he murmured, his mouth nuzzling her ear and the fine hairs that curled at her temple. He moved his hips. "See what I mean?"

Oh, God. Did she ever. Marcie clung to him and stifled a moan.

"I want you, Marcie," Ben whispered.

"Yes . . ." *And I want you, too,* Marcie thought dizzily. "But . . ."

"I know." Ben closed his eyes and held her tight. "It's too soon."

He wanted her, ached for her. Even before the kiss, he'd been drawn to her, warmed by her. Turned on by her. He had kept his distance, worked on the friendship angle, only because he had thought that was all Marcie was willing—able—to give. But now he knew better, now she had shown him . . .

Recalling the phone call, he thought bleakly, It's too late.

"We have to talk," he said, and brusquely set her away from him because he knew that if he didn't, he would never again find the strength.

He turned his back on her injured expression, on the hurt and bewilderment he saw in her eyes. "Before we can go any further," he said, his eyes on the ugly arborite table with the covered bowl of chili on top, "there is something you have to know. Something I just found out and which, I think you'll agree, could very well change everything."

"What?" Marcie couldn't imagine what he was talking about.

Ben turned. His face looked gray.

"Marcie," he said. "According to Judge Claymore, there's been a mistake. And it means that we're not . . . really married."

Chapter Ten

"Not really married?"

She was *not* Ben's wife? Marcie stared at Ben without comprehension, as if he had spoken Swahili or something instead of plain English. "I don't get it."

He had just finished telling her that thanks to some electronic snafu they would have to reappear before the judge and sign some additional paperwork before the marriage could be duly recorded. In the meantime...

"I don't understand," Marcie restated with hysteria just around the corner. "I mean, what kind of a software *glitch* is it that can render a perfectly legal ceremony suddenly null and void? I thought computers were supposed to make our lives easier...."

"Wherever did you hear *that* rumor?" Ben muttered, resorting to gallows humor when what he really felt like doing was grabbing something and throwing it at the wall.

Because as he had feared, no sooner had he passed Judge Claymore's shattering revelation on to Marcie and she was recoiling from him in shock and dismay.

"Look at the bright side," he quipped grimly when she said nothing else, just paced the floor in silent agitation. "This'll save us the hassle of getting a divorce at the end of next year."

Marcie sliced him a withering glance. "I don't think that's funny."

"Yeah, I know." Ben rubbed his brow. A headache was making itself felt. Figuring things couldn't get much worse, he added, "You want to hear something else that isn't?"

Marcie didn't answer, so Ben took her silence as assent, thinking, Might as well get the whole darned mess on the table and go for broke. He said, "Chester Hillier's at the ranch."

He had expected her to be shocked, but wasn't prepared for the kind of reaction he got.

Marcie's face went deathly white. An expression of horrified disbelief dawned in her eyes. She raised both palms and backed away from him as though to ward off a physical attack. And she whispered, "How could you?"

Her voice shook, and it turned strident with accusation as she added, "For the love of God, Ben, how could you do this to me?"

Stunned into speechlessness, Ben could only stare at her as inside him something shriveled. Love, trust, faith—all those tender fledgling emotions, barely reborn, now withered and died in the face of this, Marcie's latest show of mistrust.

He didn't say a word. In truth, he couldn't have spoken if he'd tried. But he continued to mutely gaze at her.

And in his expression Marcie belatedly recognized the harm her impetuous accusation had done. She blanched. Her hand flew to her mouth as if to contain the hurtful words after the fact.

"Oh, Ben," she whispered, her eyes and tone of voice beseeching him to believe. "Forget I said that. Please forget I said that."

She went to him. He turned away from her tentative touch. Marcie lowered her hand, saying, "I...I'm upset. I didn't think... Oh, Ben, I *know* you wouldn't..."

"You're right," Ben said, finding his voice at last and speaking more coldly than he ever had because that was the only way he could contain his incredible hurt. "I wouldn't."

Because he was human, the need to strike back was strong. Briefly he gave in to it, choosing words as his weapon. "But only because I care for your child," he said. "Not out of any particular regard for you."

Slamming his hat on his head, he scooped up his jacket and stalked out into the night on a blast of wind and swirling snow.

Left once again to stare at the door, Marcie's knees began to shake and then to buckle. She sank down on the bed. With a strangled sob, she buried her face in her hands. She sat like that for a long time, not really thinking anything but feeling...

Oh, all the things she was feeling. Regret, despair, hopelessness. Pain.

But most of all she felt a sense of loss that was all the greater for the fact that she had lost something that had been within reach, but had not yet really been hers. Something that had not yet been more than a dream, and a barely recognized one at that.

A dream of love. A love unlike the one she had known before, which she knew now hadn't been love at all. Love for a man, a strong man, a man she could lean on. A man so strong, he hadn't been afraid to lean on her, too.

Ben.

The dream of a home. A real home inhabited by a real family. A family that was made up of mother, child and father. Herself, Josie and again ... Ben.

Marcie wanted to weep for her loss but found that she had no tears. Drained and exhausted, she eventually toppled sideways and, still dressed, slept.

At first Ben had simply walked. Unmindful of direction, like a man driven by demons he had stomped along the deserted highway. He had welcomed the blizzard's cruel force for it gave him an outlet for the rage that consumed him.

A rage that was directed at himself. At his stupidity, a stupidity that had allowed him to make the same mistake twice.

Dammit, hadn't he learned? Hadn't he sworn to himself not to repeat the folly? Hadn't he vowed never to make himself vulnerable again?

To think he had actually begun to trust her. And to love her. Dear God. To *love* her! While she...

His hands formed fists. While she thought him capable not only of betrayal, not only of callously reneging on his promise of protection, but of doing so when she and the child were at their most vulnerable.

He kept walking until the need to rant and rave had been frozen out of him. And then he had gone to sit in the Bronco with the engine running and the heater going full blast before, in deference to the lateness of the hour, he had killed the motor.

It was well past midnight. Huddled into his sheepskin coat, his immediate pain and anger reduced to an overwhelming sense of disillusionment, Ben kept nodding off only to instantly jerk himself awake because of a niggling sense of unease.

The Bronco was parked several doors away from the unit Marcie occupied. His eyes grainy with fatigue, Ben peered through the frosted windshield. Except for the motel's ancient and milky neon sign, and the iridescence cast by the blanket of snow, the parking lot lay in shadowy darkness. It had stopped snowing, but the wind continued unabated, chasing the snow into eddies and drifts just as, above, billowing clouds chased each other across the sky and past the waxing crescent moon. Everything seemed quiet, and yet . . .

Frissons of alarm raised the hairs at the back of Ben's neck as he brought his face closer to the windshield and peered out.

Yes, there it was. A movement, a shifting of the shadows around the door of Marcie's room.

Ben tensed Someone was coming out of the room.

Marcie.

Ben drew back and sat bolt upright. Dammit, what harebrained scheme was the woman hatching now?

He was out of the truck and across the parking lot like a shot.

"And just where do you think you're going?" he snarled, grabbing her roughly by the arm and spinning her around.

"Nowhere. I—" Marcie closed her eyes against a wave of relief, though her heart still slammed painfully against her ribs, Ben had startled her so. "I w-was...looking f-for you. You...you'd been gone f-for so long and...it's so cold out. And—

"Oh, Ben!" she burst out, clutching at his lapels. "I'm so sorry. I didn't mean to hurt you, it's just that I'm so scared. Chester Hillier—"

"Is not quite the ogre you've always painted him to be," Ben interrupted, his tone curt. He was not inclined to let Marcie off the hook, and none-too-gently hustled her back into the room. In deference to the sleeping baby, he lowered his voice, but his tone didn't soften.

"Maybe you should try giving people a chance," he said tightly.

Releasing Marcie, his motions made jerky by his seething emotions, he unbuttoned his coat.

"Instead of always expecting the worst."

"Look, I've tried to apologize...."

"To me." With suppressed violence, Ben tossed the jacket onto the table and dropped his hat on top. "Well, I say forget about me. And forget about yourself for a change, too. You've got a child to consider, a child who has only one set of grandparents in this whole world. Chester and Jackie Hillier may not be ideal in-laws but they are Josie's *family*, Marcie, regardless of how you might feel about them. They are ready to love her. And frankly—"

With one hand on his hip, Ben glared at Marcie, punctuating each word with the stiffly pointing forefinger of his other hand. "—I, for one, don't think you have the right to deprive her of that."

"I have every right!" Marcie flared, feeling cornered, scared and ... betrayed. She was thinking it was easy for him to talk, he had nothing to lose. Whereas she ... "Darn it, Ben Kertin, I'm her mother. Widget is mine."

"She is John's, too."

"He didn't want her!"

"But his parents do. Desperately."

"Well, of course!" Though their exchange was conducted in a near whisper, it didn't lack fervor or heat. Marcie's voice was rough with both. "And haven't I been running for that very reason? Isn't that what this—" she gestured wildly with her hands "—this whole mess, what you and I are all about?"

"Yes," Ben conceded, walking a few steps before whirling to face her. "Yes, it is. But that doesn't necessarily make your reason a valid one, does it? Situations change, Marcie. People change."

"So what are you saying?" Marcie emitted a scornful snort that rendered her question rhetorical. "That the Hilliers have changed?"

"Is that so impossible?"

"Humph."

Taking in her truculent stance and mutinous expression, Ben raked a hand through his hair, then lowered it with a sigh. "Look, Marcie," he said, striving for a reasoning tone. "I have talked to the man. And I'm telling you, Chester Hillier—"

"You *what?*" About to march into the bathroom, Marcie spun with accusation once more flaming in her eyes. "So I was right!" she exclaimed, her hands curling into fists. "You *did—*"

"Say it," Ben interrupted with a renewed surge of fury, "and I'm out of here right now."

They exchanged a mutually fulminating glare. Marcie looked away first, though still visibly upset.

Ben released a harsh breath and reminded himself that there was nothing to be gained by a snarling contest.

"I spoke with Chester earlier tonight," he said, once more forcing himself to reason. "On the telephone, after I found out from Roger that he was at the ranch. It was not a long conversation and I didn't ask him a lot of questions, just enough to realize my uncle is a broken man. John's death . . ."

Ben paused, took in Marcie's closed expression and half-turned-away stance and realized that nothing he could say would garner Chester Hillier any sympathy from her at this point.

And so he changed tactics and said, with a shrug, "But then I don't have to tell you how it is, do I? You've lived them, too, are living them still, aren't you? The guilts, the regrets, the wishing you'd been given a second chance."

He stepped up to the bed and sat down, palms braced on his thighs. "Which," he continued, "if you ask me, is all Chester wants from you. A second chance. Kind of like you got from your friend Bobo Vegada."

And what I thought I had been given with you, he added mentally, bending to tug off his boots to keep from letting his disillusionment show.

"And that's all I've got to say on the subject," he told her curtly, kicking the boots aside and then stretching out on one side of the queen-size bed. "I'm bushed."

He covered his eyes with his forearm and within seconds was sound asleep.

Marcie, her heart heavy, her thoughts and emotions a maelstrom of conflict and confusion, stared down at him for several long moments before wearily resuming her trip to the bathroom. She, too, was exhausted beyond words, but she knew that sleep would not be granted her that night.

Three days later, packing her meager belongings as well as the baby's wealth of stuff preparatory to spending the Christmas holidays at the Hilliers' and prior to her permanent relocation to L.A., Marcie pondered her altered circumstances and the speed with which they had come about.

By making the decision to meet Chester Hillier halfway, she had effectively ended the cold war they had fought for as long as they had known each other. A war, she had come to realize in the course of her sleepless night at the ValeVu Motel, in which there could be no winners. Only losers.

With her child, with Josie, the biggest loser of all.

It had by no means been an easy conclusion at which to arrive. On the contrary, while lying fully clothed and stiffly apart next to the deeply slumbering Ben, she had fought against reason with everything she had.

She had recalled John's often-embittered tales of growing up lonely in boarding and prep schools, thanks to his parents' frenetic social pace and frequent absences on trips abroad.

Only to remember his other stories, too. Stories of sun-filled family summers on Martha's Vineyard. Of sailing with Chester on the family sloop. Of fishing excursions to Northern Wisconsin, and of Chester spending hours on end patiently teaching his son the finer points of tennis and golf.

So she called to mind the times the Hilliers had snubbed her, disdained her, hurt her feelings.

Only to be grudgingly forced to concede that she—and John, too, for that matter—had gone out of their way to be as flamboyant and nonconformist as possible on those rare Hillier social occasions they had bothered to attend.

All right, all right. Out of sorts with herself and her logic, Marcie had pressed her fingertips against her pounding temples and squeezed shut her gritty, burning eyes.

But what about that letter the Hilliers had sent her after John's death? she had demanded. What about that? Written by their attorney, it had been threatening in tone as well as demeaning and intentionally intimidating.

And it had been the one thing for which she could not drum up a mitigating counterargument during her nocturnal debate.

But then, Chester, in the course of their initial and mutually painful confrontation two days ago right here at the ranch, had cited, and produced copies of, several subsequent letters as proof of his, and his wife's, change of heart.

At which time Marcie had had to admit that she had destroyed each one. Unopened. Unread.

It had been difficult for her to concede that perhaps she should have taken the time to inform herself of the Hilliers' intentions, that she should have faced them head-on instead of running. And hiding.

"We heard from Rosalie James," Chester had said at one point, "that you claimed to be only six months

pregnant. And that Ben, not John, is the baby's father."

Marcie and Ben had exchanged glances at this, both
thinking, *So that's how Chester had come to know.*

It had been one of the few—no, the only—even remotely close moments Marcie and Ben had shared since
that night at the motel.

The ride back to the ranch had been nerve-racking:
a desert of strained silence punctuated by infrequent
and terse oases of stilted speech.

Nor had matters between them improved since.

Marcie stopped packing and thrust both hands into
her hair in a gesture of frustration, hurt and anger.
Damn the man. She swallowed against the painful
constriction that seemed to have taken up permanent
residence in her throat.

Outwardly cordial when the occasion required, but
otherwise as cold and remote as the man in the moon,
Ben had deflected every one of Marcie's attempts to
speak to him in private.

Damn him, she thought again. Hadn't she apolo-
gized? Not once, but again and again? Did he have to
be so *damned* thin-skinned and mule-headed?

In response to Chester's statement, Ben had—
curtly—informed his uncle that not only was he *not*
Josie's father, he was no longer even Marcie's husband.

To his credit, he had also made it clear that, should
Marcie decide not to play ball, he would not stand idly
by should Chester or his attorneys try to strong-arm or
bully her.

"I wouldn't," his uncle had assured him, as well as
Marcie. "I swear, I wouldn't..."

And Marcie, having witnessed the once-proud and arrogant Chester Hillier humble himself, had ultimately been unable to do anything but reach out to the man in a gesture of peace.

"Give us a chance," he had begged. "That's all we ask. Give us a chance to be close to this child, to demonstrate to her what we apparently failed to convey to John—that we love her. Want her. Are proud of her. Allow us to share in your lives. Please . . ."

That it cost Chester dearly to approach her like this had been painfully obvious to Marcie. And that his motives were sincere had been obvious, too. Her heart had urged her to let bygones be bygones, to make a fresh start. And, in the end, as had always been her way, she had followed the dictates of her heart.

Especially after witnessing the loving tenderness with which Chester gazed at his sleeping granddaughter.

In the course of several subsequent heart-to-heart talks—Chester had sought Marcie and the baby's company at every opportunity—and after a long telephone conversation with Jaqueline, Marcie had accepted this invitation to spend Christmas with them at their condo in Vail.

Ben, on the other hand, had declined.

Not surprisingly, Marcie reflected sadly as she pressed down the lid of the suitcase. She let her hands rest there a moment before she snapped shut the locks.

Her brief marriage to Ben was well and truly over. Ben had shown no interest in seeking out Judge Claymore or to re-sign any paperwork. More, he was making it a point never to be alone with her. In fact, as much as possible, he avoided her company altogether. With Chester quartered in the nursery-cum-guest

room, and Josie in the master bedroom with her, Ben
was bunking on the sofa in his study.

Ever since that awful moment back in the motel
room when she had, unthinkingly, questioned his integrity by once again suspecting him of conniving with
the Hilliers, he had treated her with such cold courtesy, it chilled her to the bone.

And broke her heart.

She tossed on her lonely bed at night, trying to come
up with ways in which she might penetrate his reserve
and reclaim a part, however small, of the friendship
they had come to share. She searched for ways to make
him see that the shock of hearing their marriage was
invalid had redoubled her fear of losing her child. And
that she had blindly lashed out in response to that fear.

But whatever she came up with sounded phony, defensive and lame, even to herself.

She thought of confronting him, of boldly facing
him down and demanding that he listen. And forgive.

She thought of getting down on her knees and telling him that she loved him. And to beg him to let her
stay.

But when their paths would cross, he would look at
her as though she were a stranger, and she would say
nothing. Nothing at all.

Ben dreaded those chance encounters. Almost as
much as he longed for them.

To see Marcie, who seemed to grow daily more
beautiful, go serenely about her motherly duties was at
once a joy and an agony for him. He missed the closeness with her and the child, mourned the loss of that
sense of family they had—all-too-briefly—shared. He

missed holding the baby, missed being part of Marcie's routine.

But he told himself it was best to keep away from her so that it wouldn't hurt so much when she left the ranch for good.

The loss of her, the emotional loss if not yet the actual physical one, was already filling him with more anguish than any man should have to bear.

For he loved her, loved Marcie with an intensity that far surpassed anything he had ever felt for Jane. Even in the throes of first passion, he had never ached for Jane the way he ached for Marcie. Never hungered the way he hungered now. Never needed the way he needed now.

If only she would give some sign that she felt even a fraction of what he was feeling, Ben thought as he lay night after night on that back-breaker of an office couch. He would get on his knees and beg her to stay.

But there had been no such sign. Not when she accepted Chester Hillier's olive branch or his invitation to Christmas in Vail. And not when she had come to him after Bobo Vegada's phone call, earlier today.

It had been a shock to see Marcie standing in the door of his study. For a moment, his heart had soared. But then he had looked into her shuttered face, had noted the way she avoided meeting his gaze and had clamped down hard on his wayward emotions.

"Yes?" he had forced himself to coldly inquire when she just stood there, looking at anything but him.

"I came to tell you that I—we—won't be back after Christmas."

"I see." Through a haze of acute pain, Ben observed such mundane details as the ticking of the clock, the hiss and crackle of the fire in the hearth, the on-

and-off whine of a chain saw from somewhere out-side.

With a curious detachment, he watched Marcie twist her fingers into pretzels and knots.

And though he longed to be able to say, "Stay. Please just stay," what came out was a frigid "I suppose that's for the best."

"Yes." Marcie could barely speak for the lump that closed her throat. Look at him, she thought misera-bly, sitting there so cool and collected. He doesn't care. He never cared. "Though it was kind of you to offer to let me stay."

Ben brushed that aside with an impatient jerk of the hand. "No problem. The guesthouse is yours, after all, and the renovations are almost complete."

"Yes. I've been wanting to thank you for that."

As she spoke, Marcie forced herself to look at him. Their gazes met, held. Something vibrated between them, something that turned Marcie's knees to jelly. Something that put every nerve in Ben's body on red alert.

Abruptly, simultaneously, they each looked away.

"No thanks are needed," Ben said brusquely. Rest-less, his nerves aquiver, he tapped his pencil on the desk.

"So. You'll be staying with Chester, is that it? A wise choice. He's got the means to take care of you and he's crazy about the kid."

"Yes, he is." *The kid.* Marcie's heart twisted pain-fully in her chest. That's all Widget was to him any-more, just some kid.

And she? No doubt she, too, was nothing more to Ben than just some woman. A woman he'd been kind to for a while, but whom he now no longer cared about one way or another.

"But, no, we won't be staying with Chester and Jackie beyond the holidays," she said. "I—that is, Widget and I—will be moving back to Los Angeles," she elaborated, although Ben's impatient frown made it obvious he couldn't wait to be rid of her and didn't give a damn about her plans. "Bobo called."

That got a reaction, at last. Ben's eyes widened, then narrowed and snapped to Marcie's. His face flushed.

"With another gallant proposal of marriage?" he snarled, tossing the pencil aside as though it had turned into something slimy and vile. He surged to his feet.

For a moment, Marcie was half afraid, half hoping he would charge out from behind that desk and— what? Forbid her to leave? Touch her? Grab her? Shake her?

Kiss her?

She hung her head, biting down on her lip, thinking, Yes. All of that.

But all Ben said was "Congratulations" in a tone of such disdain, Marcie's head came up smartly and she matched him glare for ferocious glare.

"For your information," she said through gritted teeth, "Bobo has offered me a job. A share in a large commission. A sculpture. It's a wonderful opportunity...."

She stopped, unable to say more because her throat had closed completely. Tears were a burning pressure at the back of her eyes and it took all of her strength to battle them back. Her eyes stayed on Ben's by sheer force of will.

Staring back at her, steeling himself against the rush of emotions that threatened to lay him low, Ben gripped the edge of his desk to keep himself from leaping across it and dragging her into his arms.

"I would have thought you'd unbend enough to at least wish me well," Marcie quietly managed at last. She turned to go but, at the door, turned to look back.

Ben hadn't moved. In truth, he doubted he could have moved just then even had his life depended on it. It was all he could do to meet her burning gaze and watch her lips form words.

"I never wanted things to end like this," she whispered in a voice so rough and shivery, Ben had to strain to understand what she said. "You were kind once, Ben. And I'll always...love you for that."

Love. Time and time again in the empty days that followed, Ben told himself that was not the word Marcie had used. He had misunderstood. He had misheard her.

She despised him, he reminded himself. Grimly adding, And rightly so. He *should have* wished her well. He *should have* unbent. He *should have* long ago learned that a grudge was a useless, an imbecilic burden for a grown man to lug around.

And now she was gone. The house was empty. Yet at the same time it was so crammed full with the essence of her that it choked him. She lurked in every room, followed his every step.

And her voice whispered to him on the wind.

You were kind once. I'll always...love you for that. ...always love you for that....love you for that. ...love you...love you...love...

Could it be? Was it possible?

Restless, lonely, Ben prowled the empty rooms. He filled himself with the scent of her that still lingered, closed his eyes and could feel her close by. But she was gone. Lost to him, thanks to his obsessive need to nurture his injured pride.

So she had suspected him of betraying her. So what? It wasn't the first time they had squared off because one of them had overreacted. They had both been hurt before, and as a consequence they had both been short on trust and long on suspicion.

She had felt cornered, the safety and well-being of her child threatened by a member of *his* family. A member with whom she knew he had been conferring.

By announcing the nullification of their marriage the way he had, he had pulled the rug out from under her completely. She had been alone once again. On her own, at least in her perception. She had been scared. Not for herself but for her baby. And why wouldn't she be? Chester's behavior had been anything but rational.

Given her frame of mind—precarious, at best, all of that day—*of course* she didn't stop to reason things out. Even if that had been her way, which it wasn't. Impulsive, emotional, with quicksilver moods, *that* was Marcie Jacobs Hillier.

Marcie Jacobs Hillier *Kertin*.

Ben stopped at a window and pressed his throbbing forehead against the frosted glass. Marcie Kertin. He had liked the sound of that. He liked it still.

The question was, did he like it enough to do what he knew he had to in order to get her to accept his name again? Which was to bare his soul to her...and risk having it destroyed.

Behind him the clock chimed once. Ben neither knew nor cared whether that indicated some half-hour mark or simply one o'clock. He was focused inward, hearing again Marcie's emotion-rough whisper.

...*always love you for that.*

Was there a chance that *love* had been the word? he wondered yet again. And if so, had she meant by that the kind of love he craved from her, the kind of love he felt *for* her?

Passionate love, possessive love of the kind that meant having and holding, forever?

And suddenly he knew that he had to find out or go out of his mind.

Marcie could see the Hilliers were trying. In their large and spacious condo, they had put her into a very comfortable room with a balcony that fronted the ski slopes. They had accommodated without comment her request that Josie be put in there with her.

They doted on the child, yet in no way tried to interfere with Marcie's schedules or edicts regarding certain do's and don'ts. They were pathetically eager to baby-sit, so much so that, in addition to her daily outings with the baby, Marcie made it a point to take a second walk in the afternoon, alone.

Alone and, though the streets bustled with an energetic and fun-loving crowd, lonely. She missed the ranch. She missed Cookie, the hands.

And always, *always* she missed Ben.

She ached for him, dreamed of him, pined for him. And no amount of playtime with her child, of convivial chats with her hosts, of brisk walks and fielding come-hither glances from sun-bronzed ski bums did anything to alleviate her incredible sense of loss.

She liked it in Vail. She had always loved to ski and, in the course of their conversations, had mentioned that to the Hilliers one night over dinner.

To her shock and dismay, the next morning, Christmas Eve Day, a troop of people marched into the condo, bearing everything from ski apparel and the latest equipment for Marcie to approve and try on.

Her protest was summarily hushed—it was Christmas, after all. And they wanted to see her happy.

Marcie could have told them that her unhappiness had nothing to do with material things and Christmas presents, but bit her tongue. Besides, in view of the joy and excitement on Chester and Jaqueline's face when they saw her trying things on, Marcie knew it would be boorish to keep arguing that this was all way too much.

That afternoon, right after lunch, instead of taking her customary solitary walk, she went skiing. Widget was napping and Jaqueline had been left with a bottle for a feeding later on that day. Much as she loved her child and motherhood, Marcie felt an exhilarating sense of freedom as she sat on the chair lift and soared toward the mountaintop.

A sort of peace overcame her as she took a deep breath and looked around. Below lay the lodge and beyond it, the Hillier condo in a setting as picturesque as a Currier and Ives Christmas card.

A merry jingle played over the public-address system and all the stately evergreens wore coats of pristine white. The sun shone brightly overhead, but without warmth. Frost nipped at cheeks and noses and made them glow.

In spite of her heartache, amid so much beauty Marcie was hard put to stifle an exuberant yodel as she schussed down the slope on her first downhill run.

Rusty after years away from the slopes, but a daredevil nevertheless, she took several spectacular, though blessedly harmless, spills. The last one quite near the base of what she had already decided would be her final run of the day. She was exhausted, but pleasantly so. It had been a wonderful afternoon. Her only regret was that she didn't have someone with whom she could have shared it.

And not just *someone*. Ben. Only Ben.

After brushing off the snow with which she was covered from her fall, she stepped out of her bindings. She was bending to pick up her skis and heft them across one shoulder for the trek home when an achingly familiar baritone offered, "Here, I'll take those for you."

Still bent, Marcie froze at the sound of that voice. And then, her motions jerky, she slowly straightened, letting her eyes travel up a pair of long, jean-clad legs, past a bulky, fawn-colored shearling coat to the haggard, but to her, infinitely handsome and dear, face of the man she loved.

"Ben." Her lips formed the name without sound. The skis dropped from her hands. Her eyes filled with tears as she stared at him, not daring to blink for fear he would disappear. One of her mittened hands reached out to touch him, to feel if he was real.

Ben caught the hand between both of his gloveless ones. "Did you mean it?" he asked, his voice rough, his gaze intent. He hadn't meant to blurt it out. All the way over here in the plane, he had practised what he would say.

But now, seeing her, *feeling* her as he all but crushed her small hand between both of his, the words sprang up from his need and tumbled out of their own volition. "When you spoke to me of...love, did you...?"

He saw her eyes widen. Saw her bite her quivering lip and give her head a hard, quick shake before she tore her gaze away.

Say it, a voice inside him urged. *You say it first, dammit. Open up to her. Take a chance.*

"You see," he said huskily, "the reason I'm asking is that I..." He took a breath, harshly released it with a rueful chuckle. "I'm not very good with pretty words but—dammit—I'm crazy in love with you, Marcie-girl."

"Oh, Ben." Marcie's hand spasmed inside his grip, and her eyes, awash now with tears and full of an incredulous sort of wonder, flew back to his.

"I've never loved anyone the way I love you," Ben said hoarsely, desperately, when she only continued to look at him in silence while tears streamed down her face. "I've been a fool. I've been a jerk. I've been—"

"Everything this foolish woman ever wanted," Marcie whispered, pressing her free hand against his lips to silence him. "And, yes, Ben, I did mean what I said. I'm grateful for all you've done for me, and I'll always love you for it."

"For my kindness?"

"Among other things," Marcie said with a misty little smile. She had never seen the oh-so-macho Benedict Kertin so unsure. So vulnerable. And because she knew what it must be costing him to let her see inside him like this, she didn't tease him, only loved him all the more.

"We still need to talk," Ben said, casting a glance at the bustling world around them. He was eager to get her alone somewhere and demonstrate his tremendous need. "Somewhere other than here."

"We are talking," Marcie said. "And here is fine."

"It's freezing cold."

"If you'd take me in your arms, we could keep each other warm."

Ben looked around once again. Skiers were everywhere, coming off the hill as darkness fell, and heading toward the brightly lit lodge. He had never been one to be demonstrative in public. And this was certainly public.

But when his gaze returned once more to Marcie's, and when he saw in them the light of love, suddenly it no longer mattered.

With a groan of need he dragged her against him and wrapped her in his arms. And then he caught her lips in a kiss so hot and urgent, it could have started a polar meltdown.

Deep, deeply, they kissed. Insatiable in their need, their tongues mated, their bodies strained. And all around them was joy and laughter. All the blessings of the season were theirs.

"Merry Christmas!" people called. "Happy Holidays!" and more.

Ben and Marcie, intent on each other, neither heard them nor cared. Their kiss ended, but they didn't draw apart.

"I love you," Marcie said.

"Marry me," Ben replied.

"I already did."

"Then marry me again. This time for good."

And Marcie did, on the day after Christmas.

* * * * *

HE'S NOT JUST A MAN, HE'S ONE OF OUR

Fabulous Fathers

FATHER BY MARRIAGE
Suzanne Carey

Investigator Jake McKenzie knew there was more to widowed mom Holly Yarborough than met the eye. And he was right—she and her little girl were *hiding* on her ranch. Jake had a job to do, but how could he be Mr. Scrooge when this family was all he wanted for Christmas?

Fall in love with our Fabulous Fathers!

Coming in December, only from

Silhouette

R O M A N C E™

FF1295

MILLION DOLLAR SWEEPSTAKES (III)

No purchase necessary. To enter, follow the directions published. Method of entry may vary. For eligibility, entries must be received no later than March 31, 1996. No liability is assumed for printing errors, lost, late or misdirected entries. Odds of winning are determined by the number of eligible entries distributed and received. Prizewinners will be determined no later than June 30, 1996.

Sweepstakes open to residents of the U.S. (except Puerto Rico), Canada, Europe and Taiwan who are 18 years of age or older. All applicable laws and regulations apply. Sweepstakes offer void wherever prohibited by law. Values of all prizes are in U.S. currency. This sweepstakes is presented by Torstar Corp., its subsidiaries and affiliates, in conjunction with book, merchandise and/or product offerings. For a copy of the Official Rules send a self-addressed, stamped envelope (WA residents need not affix return postage) to: MILLION DOLLAR SWEEPSTAKES (III) Rules, P.O. Box 4573, Blair, NE 68009, USA.

EXTRA BONUS PRIZE DRAWING

No purchase necessary. The Extra Bonus Prize will be awarded in a random drawing to be conducted no later than 5/30/96 from among all entries received. To qualify, entries must be received by 3/31/96 and comply with published directions. Drawing open to residents of the U.S. (except Puerto Rico), Canada, Europe and Taiwan who are 18 years of age or older. All applicable laws and regulations apply; offer void wherever prohibited by law. Odds of winning are dependent upon number of eligible entries received. Prize is valued in U.S. currency. The offer is presented by Torstar Corp., its subsidiaries and affiliates in conjunction with book, merchandise and/or product offering. For a copy of the Official Rules governing this sweepstakes, send a self-addressed, stamped envelope (WA residents need not affix return postage) to: Extra Bonus Prize Drawing Rules, P.O. Box 4590, Blair, NE 68009, USA.

SWP-S1195

HAPPY HOLIDAYS!

Silhouette Romance celebrates the holidays with
six heartwarming stories of the greatest gift of all—
love that lasts a lifetime!

#1120 *Father by Marriage*
by Suzanne Carey

#1121 *The Merry Matchmakers*
by Helen R. Myers

#1122 *It Must Have Been the Mistletoe*
by Moyra Tarling

#1123 *Jingle Bell Bride*
by Kate Thomas

#1124 *Cody's Christmas Wish*
by Sally Carleen

#1125 *The Cowboy and the Christmas Tree*
by DeAnna Talcott

COMING IN DECEMBER FROM

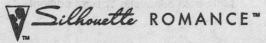

COMING NEXT MONTH

#1120 FATHER BY MARRIAGE—Suzanne Carey
Fabulous Fathers
Holly Yarborough was just another assignment, but that didn't
stop Jake McKenzie from falling for the sexy female rancher.
When Holly learned the truth, would Jake lose his new bride?

#1121 THE MERRY MATCHMAKERS—Helen R. Myers
Read Archer's children wanted a new mother and Marina Davidov
was perfect. Little did they know that years ago, she had broken
his heart—could Read give their love a second chance?

**#1122 IT MUST HAVE BEEN THE MISTLETOE—
Moyra Tarling**
In a long-ago night of passion, Mitch Tennyson had transformed
Abby Roberts's world. Now Mitch was back, and Abby felt
forgotten love mixing with the fear that he could learn the true
identity of her son....

#1123 JINGLE BELL BRIDE—Kate Thomas
Matt Walker needed a wife—fast. And sassy waitress
Annie Patterson seemed to fit the bill. With his cowboy charm
he won her hand. Could she find a way to lasso his heart?

#1124 CODY'S CHRISTMAS WISH—Sally Carleen
All Cody wanted for Christmas was a daddy—and a baby brother!
Would Ben Sloan be the right man for his mommy, Arianna? Only
Santa knew for sure!

**#1125 THE COWBOY AND THE CHRISTMAS TREE—
DeAnna Talcott**
Crystal Weston had an ideal marriage—until tragedy tore it apart.
Now her husband, Slade, had returned to town, determined to win
her back. But would the handsome cowboy still want to renew
their vows once he met the son he'd never known?

You're About to Become a *Privileged Woman*

Reap the rewards of fabulous free gifts and benefits with proofs-of-purchase from Silhouette and Harlequin books

Pages & Privileges™

It's our way of thanking you for buying our books at your favorite retail stores.

Harlequin and Silhouette— the most privileged readers in the world!

For more information about Harlequin and Silhouette's PAGES & PRIVILEGES program call the Pages & Privileges Benefits Desk: 1-503-794-2499

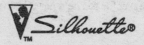

SR-PP70